FOX SWIFT

AND THE GOLDEN BOOT

Also by David Lawrence

Fox Swift
Fox Swift Takes on the Unbeatables
Anna Flowers (with Eloise Southby-Halbish)

FOX SWIFT

AND THE GOLDEN BOOT

DAVID LAWRENCE with CYRIL RIOLI

ILLUSTRATIONS BY
JO GILL

slattery
MEDIA GROUP

visit *slatterymedia.com*

foxswift.com.au

The Slattery Media Group Pty Ltd
1 Albert St, Richmond
Victoria, Australia, 3121

Text copyright © David Lawrence 2015
Illustrations © Jo Gill 2015
Design copyright © The Slattery Media Group Pty Ltd 2015
First published by The Slattery Media Group Pty Ltd 2015

All images reproduced with permission.
Flickr images: Kookaburra © Nicki Mannix, Rabbit © Esmeralda Dia

All rights reserved. No part of this publication may be reproduced, stored in a retrieval system or transmitted in any form or by any means without the prior written permission of the copyright owner. Inquiries should be made to the publisher.

National Library of Australia Cataloguing-in-Publication entry

   Creator: Lawrence, David, 1964- author.

   Title: Fox Swift and the Golden Boot / David Lawrence ; Cyril Rioli, contributor ; Jo Gill, illustrator.

   ISBN: 9780992379186 (paperback)

   Target Audience: For children.

   Subjects: Australian football--Juvenile fiction.

      Australian football teams--Juvenile fiction.

      Football stories.

   Other Creators/Contributors:

      Gill, Jo, illustrator.

      Rioli, Cyril.

   Dewey Number: A823.4

Group Publisher: Geoff Slattery
Project Manager: Courtney Nicholls
Editor: Bronwyn Wilkie
Design: Kate Slattery and Chris Downey

Printed and bound in Australia by Griffin Press

slatterymedia.com

FOX SWIFT
AND THE GOLDEN BOOT

CONTENTS

1 Sheepless Nights 7
2 Think of the Children 19
3 Plane to Sea 28
4 Tree's Company 38
5 Tiwi Pee-Wee 46
6 Pumped Up for School 58
7 Laser Show 69
8 'D' Day 80
9 A Winter's Roast 89
10 A Chocolate Surprise 101
11 Weeding Out the Problems 111
12 Coaching Secrets 121
13 Fast Changes 132
14 Oink Oink 142
15 A Tearful Ending 156
16 It's All 'Bout that Mace 170
17 Lab Rat 182
18 Cunning Like a Dingo 190
19 A Digger Departs 203
20 Two Finals and Funeral 215
21 Bank You Very Much 229
22 Case Closed 244
A Quirky Footy Dictionary 256

Dedication
This book is in loving memory of Harrison Riedel,
and is dedicated to the amazing students and teachers
on the Tiwi Islands.

1

Sheepless Nights

Fox Swift was having an amazing dream.

He was playing for the Diggers against the Dragons, and in his team were Joey the kangaroo and a giant-sized Gary the rabbit.

Fox looked on as Joey leapt over Mace Winter and pulled down a screamer, then handballed to Gary, who scampered past **on the burst**. The enormous white bunny casually kicked a 60-metre goal, and gave Fox an enthusiastic "high paw" as he hopped past.

The Dragons centre half-back Vince Brogan started clapping and called out, "Top goal, Gary!"

Mace's face went bright red as he yelled, "Shut up Vince!"

Fox smiled in his sleep.

Check out the definition of any words in **bold** in A Quirky Footy Dictionary on page 256.

Moments later, he was awoken by a faint noise. He initially mistook the sound for a mosquito, and slapped his ear really hard.

"Ouch!"

He was now wide awake, and remembered he was staying over at Mo Officer's farm.

Fox was not the only Diggers player sleeping over at Mo's—Lewis, Hugo, Paige, Rosie and Chung were also there.

They were all spending a few days of their holidays helping out the Officers, who, like most of the farmers in the area, were struggling because of the drought.

Times were very tough in the district, but this had not always been the case. Fox had learned in one of his teacher's boring history classes that Davinal had once been a very wealthy goldmining town.

He could still remember Mr Grinter explaining in his droning voice how people travelled to Davinal from all over the world with dreams of striking it rich.

Mr Grinter went on to tell the class a story about a crazy old prospector called 'Toothy' Taylor. Everyone called him Toothy as a joke—because he had no teeth at all. Anyway, Toothy Taylor rode into town one day claiming he had discovered the largest gold nugget in the world. The townspeople were very excited by this news until Toothy explained to them how he had made his discovery.

"My horse Betsy spoke to me, and she told me where to dig!" said the toothless old-timer.

The townspeople were suddenly less excited about Toothy Taylor's discovery, because they realised he was completely bonkers! Unfortunately for old Toothy, he had a massive heart attack while celebrating at the local hotel that evening, and dropped dead on the spot.

"Not surprisingly, no one ever found Toothy Taylor's nugget," said Mr Grinter.

"They should have asked his horse!" called out Lewis, causing the class to burst out laughing.

But the gold rush days had ended well over 100 years ago and Davinal was no longer a wealthy district. Many farmers had recently been forced to move off the land because they could no longer support their families.

The Officers had so far managed to hang on to their farm, but they owed the bank a lot of money and were struggling financially. That's why Fox and his friends had volunteered to help out.

With his ear still ringing from when he had slapped himself, Fox tried to go back to sleep. It had been a long, hard day working on the farm, but he had enjoyed every second of it. He and his friends had started off by feeding the chooks and collecting the eggs. Fox had been about to enter the chicken coop through a small wire gate when Lewis stopped him and said with a smile, "Sorry mate, your kind aren't allowed in here!"

No Foxes in the Hen House

Lewis then crouched down in the corner of the coop and started making clucking noises. He got louder and louder before stopping all of a sudden, and then giving one final "Berkerk!" and standing up to reveal two freshly laid chicken eggs.

"I'm not touching those ones," laughed Fox.

Chung then put on a quick magic show by pulling an egg out of Paige's ear and another from Rosie's pocket. He then started coughing as if he had something caught in his throat. Fox had no idea how he did it, but Chung somehow managed to pull three eggs out of his mouth, one at a time. After the third egg came out, he let out a small burp and took a bow.

Chung's friends gave him a huge round of applause while the chooks stared at them as if they were all mad.

When they dropped off the eggs to Mrs Officer in the kitchen, Lewis said, "You might want to give those a rinse!"

They then let the Officers' two blue heeler sheepdogs (Johnny and Cash) off their chains and made sure they had water, swept out the dusty shearing shed, helped Mo mend some fences and collected a month's worth of firewood.

But Fox's favourite farmyard chore had been feeding bales of hay to the sheep from the back of the ute. The sheep would chase madly after the vehicle, baa-ing thankfully as Fox and his friends tossed out handfuls of hay. But the coolest thing about it was that Mo was driving the ute.

"Ownonthfrmntonthrod," Mo had explained.

"He's only allowed to drive the ute around the farm and not on the road," translated Paige. Fox had no idea how Paige, or anyone for that matter, understood a word Mo said, because he barely opened his mouth when he spoke.

Mo had grown taller since the end of the footy season, and Fox didn't think it was possible, but he now looked even more like his dad. Luckily, Mr Officer had grown a moustache—from a distance it was the only way you could tell them apart.

Fox felt sorry for the full-forwards who would be playing against the Diggers this season, because Mo was not only taller, he was even stronger than last year. The young farm boy would casually pick up a hay bale in each arm, and calmly lob them onto the back of the truck. Meanwhile Fox and Lewis could barely manage to lift one bale between the two of them!

Lewis shook his head and said, "The only difference between Mo and the Incredible Hulk, is that the Hulk is green … and Mo is 10 times stronger!"

Mo smiled at Lewis and said, "Bitlistokinanabitmorliftin!"

"And the Hulk is a little easier to understand," added Lewis under his breath.

Fox chuckled to himself in bed, as he started to drift back off to sleep. While he lay there he thought back to the kick-to-kick he and his friends had played in the paddock before dinner. He was super impressed that Mo could kick a perfect **torpedo punt** dead straight over 50 metres—in his work boots!

Paige, Rosie and Chung had never been taught to kick a torpedo, so Hugo carefully explained, step by step, how it was done.

"Hold the ball on an angle across your body. If you're a right-footer your left hand should be slightly forward on the footy, with the right hand behind the lacing. Guide the ball down with the right hand onto your foot at the same angle you were holding it. When the outside of your foot makes contact with the ball it should spin in a spiral motion—just like a torpedo—which gives it the extra distance."

Fox smiled. Hugo was a great teacher and two minutes later Paige, Rosie and Chung were kicking torpedoes, spiralling perfectly through the air. Unfortunately for Hugo, while he was an excellent instructor, his own torpedo punts tended to fly off the side of his boot.

While Hugo was off retrieving his miskicks, Lewis entertained everyone by pretending to be a football commentator as he kicked pellets of sheep poo.

"Ohhhh that was a *crappy* kick by Rioli, he is really *stinking* it up out there. There's a good chance he'll be *dumped* from the team and this will be a big *stain* on his career."

After the kick-to-kick, the Diggers teammates took turns riding on the Officers' two motorbikes. Hugo was up for the challenge, but somehow managed to fall from each of them.

"I need four wheels," he said to Mo as he dusted himself down. "How come you guys don't have a quad bike?!"

"Thinuneedatewheelermat," replied Mo, and Paige and Rosie burst out laughing.

"He said, 'I think you need an eight-wheeler, mate!'" translated Rosie, which caused Fox and Lewis to crack up, too.

"Oh, that is sooooo hilarious Mo," said Hugo sarcastically, making everyone laugh again.

Despite his problems kicking torpedoes and staying on motorbikes, Fox had never seen Hugo in such a great mood—no doubt because he had received some wonderful news from his doctor: he was no longer allergic to grass! This meant he was allowed to help out on Mo's farm, and even better, he wouldn't need to wear his special bodysuit when he played for the Diggers this year.

Hugo was also very pleased that his parents had given him a detective kit for Christmas, complete with a fake moustache and a magnifying glass. His hero was Sherlock Holmes, and he secretly wanted to open his own detective agency and solve puzzling crimes one day.

Fox was finally about to fall asleep when he heard that annoying buzzing noise again. He opened his eyes and concentrated. Mo was snoring, so Fox had to wait and listen in between the noisy snorts.

"There it is again," thought Fox. "What is it … a motorbike?"

Fox pulled back the sheets, quietly jumped out of bed and crept over to the window. He peered outside into the darkness searching for answers. A very strong wind had come up overnight and the tall gum trees moved wildly, like giants with ants in their pants.

Fox angled his head and listened again. Nothing.

"Must have been the wind," he thought to himself as he hopped back into bed and rested his head on the pillow.

A sudden burst of activity in the bedroom caused Fox to wake up immediately. The sun was up and people seemed to be running everywhere around him.

"What's going on?" he asked urgently.

"Shegtoutfanorpadik!" said Mo as he ran out of the room.

"The sheep have escaped from the far north paddock," translated Paige as she darted past the door of the bedroom the boys were sleeping in.

Fox quickly pulled on his jeans, a top and some runners and raced outside. Mr Officer sped off in the ute with

Paige, Rosie and Chung in front and Johnny and Cash in the back. Mo took Hugo on one of the motorbikes and Fox drove Lewis on the other.

Even from a long way away, Fox could work out what had happened. The extreme wind had obviously blown over some fence posts, and the sheep had escaped, spilling out onto the highway that ran alongside the farm.

Fox quickly brought the motorbike to a halt next to the ute, and he and Lewis leapt off so they could help herd the sheep off the road and back into the property. But before they had taken two steps a bright orange station wagon came speeding around the corner. When he saw the sheep, the driver slammed on the brakes and violently swung the steering wheel to the left.

The car spun off the road and into a ditch with an almighty thump!

The airbags immediately burst open, and the front of the car started hissing like a giant snake.

Fox ran towards the car and, seeing there was a young boy in the passenger seat, opened the door, undid the seatbelt and carefully eased him out onto the side of the road.

Mr Officer helped the dazed driver out from the other side of the car and sat him down next to the flattened fence. Both looked shaken but fortunately neither of them were hurt.

A sheep, completely unaware of the problems he and his woolly friends had caused, stared at Fox and went, "Baaaaaa."

Eventually a tow truck arrived to take away the badly damaged station wagon, and Mrs Officer offered to drive the man and his son back to their home on the other side of Davinal.

Before Mrs Officer left, Fox overheard her talking to Mr Officer.

"Bruce, do you think maybe we should take that offer and sell the farm to Selim Properties?"

Fox knew about Selim Properties because he had seen their ads on local TV offering to buy struggling farms around Davinal for small amounts of money. Their business slogan was: "We're a Farmer's Best Friend". Many of the farmers, whose land was dry and barren because of the drought and who owed the bank a lot of money, had been thankful to Selim Properties for buying them out.

"Wilberiteluv," said Mr Officer, giving his wife a hug.

With the help of the two energetic blue heelers, the Diggers players rounded up all the sheep and took them to another paddock where they couldn't escape. They then helped Mr Officer put the fence back up, and this time Mo and his father made sure the posts were so securely in place that even a cyclone couldn't knock them down.

While they were repairing the fence, Fox looked around and spotted Hugo crouching down about 20 metres away. He appeared to be inspecting some tyre marks on the ground.

"Mmmm," said Hugo, before taking a small pad from his back pocket and scribbling down some notes.

Hugo then went over and looked very closely at a fence post. He pulled out a magnifying glass from inside his jacket and held it up to the post. Fox watched him reach down and pick up a piece of wire from the ground and study it closely.

"Mmmm," he said again, jotting down a few more notes.

Fox wandered over to his super smart friend.

"What is it?" he asked.

"Maybe nothing," Hugo replied. "Maybe nothing."

2

Think of the Children

The next morning Miles Winter sat at his kitchen table in his silk dressing gown with the initials 'MW' on the breast pocket. In front of him were the tablets he took each day to try to make himself look and feel better.

He had tablets to make him more intelligent, tablets to make his hair grow back, and even tablets to make his breath smell better. None of them seemed to be working.

"Don't forget to take an extra anti-farting one!" called out Mrs Winter from the living room. "Seriously, I'm going to have to start wearing a peg on my nose!"

Mr Winter reluctantly picked up a charcoal-coloured tablet, popped it into his mouth and helped it down with a sip from an expensive-looking bottle of mineral water.

"Maybe we should get a dog," he thought, "then I could blame it for any bad smells."

Although he wasn't smiling, Miles was in a very good mood. After all the trouble he had been in last year, he had worked very hard to show everyone he was a changed man.

Even after he had completed Judge Trudy's three-month sentence of cleaning up the side of the highway on Saturdays, Miles had continued to go out and voluntarily pick up rubbish on weekends. It had become common for people driving into town to see Miles and his metal detector searching for cans that had been flung from car windows.

"It's all about the environment," he said with his hand on his heart at a recent Town Hall meeting. "If you're not part of the solution, then you're part of the problem."

Although a number of people in the Town Hall that day were still suspicious of Miles, there were also a few who nodded with approval at his words.

As part of his transformation into a model citizen, Miles had become deeply interested in Davinal's history. He was often seen spending time at the local historical centre, looking up old books and taking notes. When Mrs Savage, the centre's librarian asked him where this sudden interest had come from, he replied, "The more I know about this town's past, the more I can help it in the future."

Hugo had been in the centre at the time, and he told Fox he had nearly thrown up when he heard this. He also said that by the look on Mrs Savage's face, she felt just as sick!

After taking a tablet that claimed it would "reduce earwax by up to 38%", Mr Winter picked up the *Davinal Digest* and slowly turned the pages. He stopped when he spotted an article about the orange station wagon's accident outside the Officers' farm. As he read the story, he shook his head and muttered, "Tch, tch, tch."

Putting down the newspaper, he called out to his wife, "Mercedes, can you please pass me the phone?"

Mrs Winter walked all the way in from the living room and was annoyed to discover that the phone was on the bench, less than a metre away from her husband.

She rolled her eyes, snatched up the phone and plonked it down in front of him.

"You have got to be kidding me—" she started.

"Uh, uh, uh" said Miles, holding up his hand to cut off his wife, "a bit of shush, please—I have a very important call to make."

Mr Winter pushed a well-worn number on his speed dial and the phone at the Triple D radio station began to ring.

Shazza: Hi, you're speaking to Shazza and Bazza.

Miles: Hello, it's Miles P. Winter the Second here—

Shazza and Bazza: (audible groan)

Miles: Sorry, what was that?

Bazza: Nothing Miles, please tell us why you're ringing today.

Miles: Well Barry, may I call you Barry?

Bazza: No!

Miles: Oh, well, Bazza, I'm ringing because I am outraged—

Shazza: You're *always* outraged Miles. What's your beef today?

Miles: Well Sharon, may I call you Sharon?

Shazza: No!

Miles: Okay Shazza, I'm ringing about those sheep

that caused the accident on the highway yesterday—

Bazza: Fortunately no one was hurt—

Miles: But Bazza, people *could* have died. *Children* could have died. We have to think about the *children*!

Shazza: So, Miles, what do you think should happen?

Miles: Well Shazza, farmers who can't control their stock should be fined and sent to jail—

Bazza: Come on, Miles, there were freak winds and—

Miles: I'm just glad no one lost their lives ... at times like these you think about your own family **sniff** ... we've got to think of the *children!*

At this point Bazza pushed a button in the studio that played the sound of a heavenly choir singing, "Ahhhhhh".

Miles: What's that sound?

Shazza: Nothing. It's just that you sound like a reformed man Miles—

Miles: Reformed? I never really did anything wrong. I mean, there have just been a few misunderstandings—

Bazza: Misunderstandings?! Miles, didn't you evict a little old lady from her home while she was in a coma?

Shazza: And then tried to fleece her out of an inheritance!

Miles: Of course it sounds bad when you say it like that, but really it was ... umm ... just a ... err ...

Bazza: A complete *rip-off*?

Miles: Yes, a complete rip—no! Let's just agree that

mistakes were made by both sides and we're all moving forward. But today I want to focus on irresponsible farmers—

Shazza: So, Miles, are you saying the farmer concerned *deliberately* let his sheep out onto the highway?

Miles: Who's to say, Shazza? The drought can do strange things to farmers. But what we need to do here, is think about the *animals*—

Sound Effect: Heavenly choir

Bazza: Speaking of animals, Miles, let's talk about the Dragons—what happens to your footy team now it's suspended from the competition?

Miles: The children shouldn't suffer for a minor mistake that I made—

Sound Effect: Heavenly choir

Shazza: Are you sure it was a "minor mistake", Miles?

Miles: Yes it was Shazza, it was just a—

Shazza and Bazza: Misunderstanding!

Sound Effect: Heavenly choir

Miles: According to the rules we can re-enter the team under a different name—

Bazza: *coughing* Loophole!

Miles: What?

Bazza: Nothing, just a bit of a cough.

Miles: I just want to make things right *for the children*—

Sound Effect: Heavenly choir

Miles: Could you please stop playing that music?

Shazza: Sure, my finger keeps slipping on the button—won't happen again.

Miles: As I was saying, *the children are our future*—

Sound Effect: Heavenly choir

Shazza: Oops, my finger slipped again!

Miles: I'm not doing this for myself—

Sound Effect: Heavenly choir

Shazza: Ooops!

Mercedes: (in background) Miles, have you taken that extra anti-farting tablet yet? I'm going to have to open some windows in here.

Miles: Shush! I'm on the radio!

Bazza and Shazza: Hahahaha!

Bazza: Well we'd better let you *clear the air* with Mrs Winter, Miles.

Shazza: Yeah, smell ya later, Miles!

Miles: But, but—

click

Fox was back home packing a small suitcase in his bedroom. He had been listening to Shazza and Bazza on his clock radio, and was furious at Mr Winter for trying to cause trouble for the Officers.

"Think of the children!" he said in a high-pitched voice, mimicking Mr Winter.

However, it was hard for Fox to stay angry for long, because he was so excited. Tomorrow he and his family were going on a special holiday with Lewis, Jimmy and their parents to the Tiwi Islands!

The Tiwi Islands, which are part of the Northern Territory, are located about 100 kilometres north of Darwin. All the Riolis had been born there, and Mr and Mrs Rioli had invited the Swifts to come with them when they'd decided to take their family back for a visit.

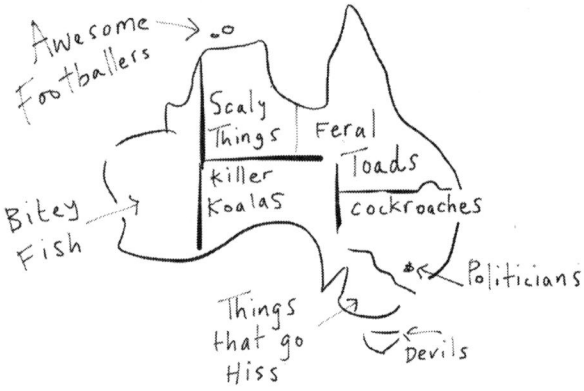

Chase was packing in his room across the hall, and Fox heard him start chanting "Tiwi, Tiwi …"

If anything, Chase was even more excited about the trip than Fox. Jimmy Rioli had told Chase how popular footy was on the Tiwi Islands and that was all he could talk about at the dinner table that evening.

"Apparently *everyone* plays football there," he said, "even the pet dogs!"

The rest of the family tried to keep a straight face.

"The *dogs* play football? Are you sure about that Chase?" asked Mrs Swift.

"Yep," said Chase confidently.

"So, Chase, if a dog kicks the ball over the boundary line, is it 'out of *hounds* on the full'?" asked Mr Swift.

"Yeah, I wonder if they win an award for *bark* of the day?" said Fox.

"And do they get dragged by the coach for playing *paw*-ly Chase?" asked Mrs Swift.

"Actually it all makes sense now," said Fox, "because the name of the Tiwi Islands full-forward is 'Al Sation'!"

"You guys are *not* funny," said Chase, trying his best not to laugh but failing miserably.

3

Plane to Sea

Fox had no idea his dad had a fear of flying.

But as they were all waiting to board the plane to Darwin, Mr Swift gave out some subtle hints. Firstly, he was unusually quiet, hardly uttering a word to anyone. Secondly, he started breathing deeply into a brown paper bag. Thirdly, and most tellingly, while they were lining up to board the plane he suddenly blurted out, "I'm *really* scared of flying!"

Chase tried to cheer his father up.

"Don't worry, Dad. If the plane crashes, we'll have a nice, soft landing on the ocean. Of course, you'll have to keep an eye out for sharks."

"That's ridiculous, Chase," said Mrs Swift, giving her husband's hand a reassuring squeeze. "We don't fly over the ocean on the way to Darwin—we'd probably crash in the desert."

Mr Swift went even paler. "Thanks, honey," he said, "I feel so much better now."

Fox soon discovered he loved flying almost as much as his dad hated it. He especially enjoyed the climb into the clouds, which made him feel like the plane was being swallowed by a giant piece of cotton wool.

He was sitting next to Lewis, and because the flight took more than four hours, they got to watch two really cool superhero movies. In between films, Lewis entertained all the passengers around them by doing impersonations of the captain making announcements.

"Hello, this is your captain speaking," he said in a deep voice. "I don't want to cause any panic, but has anyone seen my seeing-eye dog?"

Everyone burst out laughing except for Mr Swift, who shut his eyes and clenched the arm of his seat so hard Fox thought it might snap off.

The first thing to welcome them to the Northern Territory was a blast of heat as soon as they stepped off the plane. Fox instantly thought how tough it would be to play footy here, because the hot and humid weather would sap even the fittest player's strength.

The Swifts and the Riolis walked over to a small terminal on the other side of the airport, where they would board the two smaller planes that would take them across to the Tiwi Islands.

Before leaving Davinal, the airline had asked them all to email through how much they weighed. This was so the pilots could calculate exactly how many people and how much luggage could safely fly on each plane. Just to be thorough, the first thing the pilots did when the two families arrived was to weigh everyone again.

All the weights that had been emailed through were 100 per cent accurate—except for Mr Swift's.

"Must have had a *tiny* bit more Christmas pudding than I thought," he said, patting his stomach.

"*10 kilograms* worth of pudding, Dad?" teased Fox, pointing to the scales.

There were two pilots waiting to take them on the 80km flight. The Riolis' pilot was a neatly dressed, middle-aged man called Tom who led them on to the tarmac and over to their very small aircraft.

The Swifts' pilot introduced himself as 'Knackers'. He had wild green eyes, messy brown hair and his untucked shirt was covered in food stains. He led Fox and his family over to their plane, which was even smaller than the Riolis'.

"You have got to be kidding me!" said Mr Swift. "That thing's half the size of the kombi!"

To make matters worse, Knackers looked up at the sky and said, "Looks like a storm's coming in, so get set for a bumpy ride."

Mr Swift looked suspiciously at Knackers. He thought he looked more like an escapee from a lunatic asylum than a pilot.

"Don't take this the wrong way, mate, but can I see your pilot's licence?"

Knackers laughed and said, "Ah, we have a joker in the group! Just for that we're going to do a few loop the loops."

"Excellent!" said Chase and went to give Knackers a high five, but Mr Swift quickly grabbed his son's arm.

"Please don't encourage him, Chase," he said.

To Mr Swift's dismay, Knackers insisted that he sit up the front of the plane, where the pilot would be able to "keep an eye on him".

When they were in the air Knackers looked over at Mr Swift and joked, "Can you take the wheel for a sec, champ? I just want to take a quick nap."

Knackers thought this was hilarious until Mr Swift vomited all over him. After that he hardly spoke another word.

They hadn't been flying long before Fox could see the landing strip in the distance. From far away it looked like a dirt road, but as they got closer ... it still looked like a dirt road.

Knackers skilfully lined up the narrow runway and executed a perfect landing, then taxied the plane over to where the Riolis' aircraft had parked.

Waiting for them was the headmaster of Tiwi College, Mr Ian Jones, who was a great friend of Mr Rioli's. The two families were going to stay the night at the school and then get a lift north to a place called Pularumpi in the morning, which was where Lewis and Jimmy were born.

Mr Jones helped load their bags into a four-wheel drive the size of a mini bus (which he called a "troupy"), and the two families waved goodbye to the pilots as they flew off. Fox noticed that Knackers didn't wave back, and correctly guessed it was because he was still upset about Mr Swift throwing up all over him.

"With all those other stains on his shirt, I'm surprised he even noticed," said Mr Swift, whose good humour had returned now that his feet were back on the ground.

Everyone then got in the troupy and they set off for Tiwi College. As he drove, Mr Jones explained that Tiwi College was a boarding school. Kids from all over the island came there during the week and went home to their families on the weekend.

He looked in the rear-view mirror and said, "It's footy training tonight. Not sure if you young blokes play, but if you want to—"

"Yes please!" said Fox and Chase together before Mr Jones could finish his sentence.

Mr Jones dropped them off at the school's visitors' accommodation. This was a series of small one-room apartments that looked like the cargo crates you see on big ships, except each of these had a door and a window.

"They're called dongers," explained Mr Jones.

"Dongers?" said Chase, trying not to laugh. "That sounds like a rude word!"

"What do you mean?" asked Mr Jones.

"Well, you know ... if you get hit in your *donger* it really hurts—"

"That's quite enough, Chase!" interrupted Mrs Swift. "I'm very sorry, Ian."

"That's all right," said Mr Jones. "It is a pretty funny-sounding word. Now, why don't you boys get changed and I'll take you over to footy training?"

Fox, Chase and Jimmy quickly changed into their footy gear, but Lewis decided he would just watch from the boundary line.

As soon as they arrived at the large football ground, which was located right next to the main school buildings, Fox spotted groups of young footballers having a kick by the side of the oval.

His eyes were immediately drawn to one particular footballer, who had the most perfect kicking action he had ever seen. Every drop punt that came off this player's boot travelled perfectly end over end, hitting a teammate square on the chest each time. Left foot or right foot: the result was always the same.

"Who's that?" asked Fox, turning to Mr Jones.

"Her name is Jess," he replied.

The second thing Fox noticed was the variety of AFL jumpers the kids were wearing. No one club's jumper dominated—there were as many Gold Coast and Greater Western Sydney jumpers as there were of Collingwood and Essendon. In fact, he spotted every single AFL club jumper on display. Fox, who just loved footy and didn't barrack for any one AFL team, thought this was pretty cool.

Mr Jones took the three boys over to meet one of the Tiwi College teachers who coached the boys' footy team.

"Fox, Lewis and Chase, this is Mr Tipuamantimirri."

Seeing the bewildered looks on the boys' faces, Mr Tipuamantimirri smiled and said, "Just call me 'Tippa'."

"Thanks," said a very relieved Chase. "I'm not very good at saying words with more than two silly bulls."

"Silly bulls?" asked Tippa, confused.

"He means *syllables*," explained Fox.

Mr Jones told the boys that Tippa was also captain of the Tiwi Island team, the Tiwi Bombers.

"How cool would it be to have a teacher who was star footballer?" said Fox.

"Yeah," said Chase, "all we've got is Mr Percy and Mr Grinter!"

Fox was amazed at how friendly all the kids were. Within the first minute he had been given a warm welcome by Robert, Ryan, Ethan, Dion, Mark, Alexis, Stanley, John, Peter, Cedric, Emilio, Clinton, Desmond, Brandan and a kid whose name was Maurice but who everyone called 'Junior'.

The reason they called him Junior was that he, like Lewis and Jimmy, was related to Cyril Rioli, and 'Junior' was also the Hawthorn star's nickname.

Fox asked the boys what was the furthest they had travelled to play footy, and was surprised to hear that every year they flew down and played footy against a big private school in his state.

"And we always beat them!" Junior said proudly.

The football skills on display were very impressive.

Whenever the Tiwi boys got an awkward bounce, they would tap the ball forward and all of a sudden it would sit up perfectly for them to gather. Fox, Chase and Jimmy could not keep the smiles from their faces.

As always, Lewis kept everyone entertained by shouting out encouragement from the sidelines. Because he yelled out in so many different accents, it seemed like there was a huge crowd watching.

Fox liked Lewis' Scottish accent the best.

"Foox Swift, ya hafta kick the bool betta than thart luddie—I'll hafta send the Loch Ness Munsta oot aft'ya! I'd come oot thare meself, but I'm not wearing anythin' under me kilt."

After a while, Tippa called in all the players and announced the next drill.

"We're going to do some shadow runs," he said.

"Yes!" shouted all the Tiwi kids at once.

"What's a shadow run?" whispered Chase to his brother, but Fox didn't have a clue either.

Fortunately, Tippa explained exactly what he wanted them to do.

"First, line up shoulder to shoulder," he said, and everyone immediately raced into position so that they were all standing side by side in a line.

"Now I want you to run together in a line to the first cone and back," said Tippa, pointing to a cone about

50 metres away. "Then you'll run to the second cone and back, and then to the third cone and back."

Fox guessed that the second and third cones were about 100 and 150 metres away.

"Remember, you must stay in a straight line—no one can go ahead of anyone and no one can drop behind," said Tippa. "If I see the line isn't straight, you'll have to come back to the start and do it all over again."

Fox smiled. He understood that this meant the faster runners would need to slow down and the slower runners would have to push themselves to keep up.

"What a great way to make everyone think as team," he thought.

The group managed to stay in a very straight line by talking to each other as they ran. If a player started to edge ahead or fall behind, a teammate would urge them to adjust their pace.

Fox loved this drill and decided he would tell his coach, Mr Scott, all about it at the start of the season.

At the end of the most enjoyable training session of his life, Fox said goodbye to his new Tiwi College friends.

"You should play a game with us sometime," said Junior.

In his heart Fox knew he would never get to play on the Tiwi Islands, but at that moment it was something he wanted to do more than anything else in the world.

4

Tree's Company

It was a very early start the next morning, but on the plus side, Fox saw the most spectacular sunrise he had ever seen.

From out of the darkness, a glowing band of red appeared on the horizon. This red strip gradually widened, slowly transforming into streaks of dark orange, yellow and pink. The sun, looking like a gigantic egg yolk, seemed to grow from the ground, and as it moved higher the sky turned a brilliant blue.

"Wow!" said Chase. "How come we don't get sunrises like this in Davinal?"

"How do you know we don't?" asked Mr Swift. "You're never up early enough to check!"

Fox laughed. His dad was right, Chase loved his sleep. He had once managed to sleep through a very stormy night, during which a tree had crashed through his window and his bedroom had completely flooded!

Whenever the family brought up this story, Chase would say, "Hey, don't laugh! I could have drowned!"

At 7am the Riolis and the Swifts piled into Mr Jones' troupy and headed up the long, bumpy dirt road that led to Pularumpi. Lewis and Jimmy were keen to visit the local school, because they had gone there when they were very young. Fox and Chase were very keen to see it, too, because it was also where Cyril Rioli had gone to school.

They arrived at the school and walked in to find all the kids were sitting down outside the classrooms listening to the headmistress. When they spotted the visitors, a couple of young Pularumpi students got up, walked over to their visitors and gave them a hug.

"Tiwi kids have got to be the friendliest in the world," said Fox.

"Yep," said Lewis. "Imagine if visitors just dropped into our school—Mace and Vince would throw rocks at them!"

After leaving the Pularumpi school they went around to Lewis and Jimmy's Aunt Jessie's place, where they would be staying for the rest of their time on the island. Jessie had two adult sons called Michael and Phil, who straight away offered to take Lewis and Fox shooting.

"Shooting?" said Fox. "Like with a gun?"

The older boys looked surprised and stared at Fox like there was something wrong with him. "How else are we supposed to go shooting?" they asked.

Mr Rioli explained to Mr Swift that many of the kids on the Tiwi Islands go hunting with guns from a young age, and that they were all very conscious about safety.

"And we'll just be shooting at cans," added Michael.

"And I'll be driving," said Phil, looking over at Fox with a smile and adding, "in a car."

Mr Swift thought about it and said that Fox could go as long as he didn't do any shooting or get in the way, and did everything Michael and Phil told him.

Of course, Chase said he wanted to go too, but Mr Swift said he was too young.

"But, Daaad—that is soooo unfair!" whined Chase. "How come I never get to go anywhere?"

"You are on the Tiwi Islands," pointed out Mrs Swift, completely ruining Chase's argument.

So Phil drove Michael, Fox and Lewis to a secluded spot out in the bush where the two brothers set up set up Coke and Fanta cans for target practice and took turns shooting. Fox was amazed at how accurate they were. There would be a loud "Bang!" and without fail a can would go flying into the air.

Suddenly, Fox heard a kind of snorting sound that reminded him a bit of Mo Officer's snoring. Turning to stare in the direction of the noise, he was horrified to see a giant water buffalo burst through the trees.

"I'm not an expert on water buffalo moods," whispered Lewis, "but this guy does *not* look happy."

"Don't worry," said Phil, who was holding the gun. "I'll fire a warning shot over its head and he'll run off back into the bush."

He took aim and pulled the trigger. But instead of the expected "Bang!", there was a click.

"Uh oh, it's jammed!" said Phil. "Run!"

The water buffalo must have understood English, because he was the first one to start running—straight at Fox.

Phil, Michael, and Lewis instinctively clambered up nearby trees to safety. Unfortunately Fox had no instincts whatsoever when it came to water buffalos, and he ran straight for the car.

"Not the car, man! Please, not the car!" shouted Phil.

But it was too late. Fox got to the car seconds before the massive beast with the fearsome horns. He managed to jerk open the door and slide onto the seat just as the water buffalo collided with the vehicle.

Thump! The water buffalo hit the car so hard it nearly rolled over. Thump! Thump! Thump! It crashed into the side of the car three more times before finally losing interest and slowly trotting back off into the scrub.

Lewis, Phil and Michael jumped down from the trees and went over to make sure Fox was okay.

"I can't believe you jumped inside the car!" laughed Michael.

"Yeah, I can't believe you jumped inside the car either," said Phil, less amused.

When Fox got out and inspected the massive dents left by the water buffalo, he was pretty happy he was *inside* and not *outside* the car.

The next day, Michael and Phil decided to take all the younger boys hunting for mud crabs.

"Don't worry," said Phil to Mr Swift, "there are no water buffalos where we'll be going today."

Chase, although thrilled that he and Jimmy were allowed to tag along this time, was disappointed to hear this.

"Awww, now I'll never get charged by a water buffalo!" he muttered.

Phil and Michael took the four younger boys to a river lined with mangroves. From the boot of the battered car, they took out several mud crab traps, called pots. Into each of these round, netted baskets the boys put the bait—a small piece of fish they had caught earlier with a handline. Phil and Michael then placed the pots in the spots they said were certain to be swarming with crabs.

"It won't be long before we have three or four good-sized ones," promised Michael.

Fox found it very peaceful sitting by the side of the river waiting for the crabs to stroll into the traps. He shut his eyes and was almost asleep when he heard a loud splash. His eyes opened, then nearly popped out of his head. In the water, barely three metres away, was a crocodile.

"Don't worry," said Phil, "I'll take care of this."

He pulled at out his gun, pointed it just in front of the crocodile and pulled the trigger.

"Click."

"Oh no, not again!" yelled Phil. "Run!"

The four-metre-long crocodile moved with surprising speed. Fox and Chase only just managed to leap out of the way as the crocodile lunged in between them. Michael, Phil, Lewis and Jimmy sprinted off, and once again climbed the nearest trees. The crocodile then spun back around so that Fox and Chase were trapped between it and the water. The giant scaly creature started moving towards them, and, in a panic, Fox and Chase dived off the bank and into the water.

"Not the water, man! Not the water!" shouted Phil.

The crocodile almost seemed to smile. He couldn't believe his prey had made it so easy for him. He gently eased his gigantic body into the river.

"Get behind me, Chase," said Fox, who had never been so frightened in his life.

The crocodile was less than two metres away from them when Michael, Phil, Lewis and Jimmy suddenly started splashing the water back near the bank. They jumped up and down and shouted, making as much noise as possible. Lewis even grabbed the giant reptile's tail.

This made the crocodile really angry, and it turned around and started snapping furiously at the four boys on the shore. This clever diversion gave Fox and Chase time to get out of the water and scramble up the nearest tree.

Meanwhile Lewis, Jimmy, Michael and Phil all leapt into trees narrowly avoiding the vicious crocodile's powerful jaws. Fox was amazed to hear them shrieking with laughter. He was actually surprised he could hear anything at all, because his heart was beating so loudly.

Fox looked at his brother and said, "Welcome to the Tiwi Islands, Chase."

They both shook their heads and laughed.

They all watched the crocodile stomp angrily back towards the water and swim away. Lewis, Jimmy, Michael and Phil jumped down from their trees.

"Are you guys coming down?" Phil asked Chase and Fox.

"Not for a long time," said Fox.

"Okay, you stay up there with the yellow tree snake," said Michael.

"With the yellow *what*?" cried Chase.

Fox slowly turned his head to left. Sure enough, a giant snake was slithering towards them.

"Ahhhhhhhhhhhhh!" they yelled, jumping from the tree.

Their four friends fell down laughing.

5

Tiwi Pee-Wee

That night, after Aunty Jessie had cooked a delicious meal of the fresh mud crabs caught that day, the boys left the table and went to sit around a small fire at the back of the house.

"There are so many scary creatures on the Tiwi Islands," said Chase.

"Yesterday there was a water buffalo, today a crocodile and a yellow tree snake—what are we going to see tomorrow?"

"There's one creature on the island you haven't seen yet, Chase," said Phil, winking at Michael, "and it's the scariest one of them all."

Chase's eyes widened.

"What is it? A scorpion? A lion? A piano fish?"

Fox rolled his eyes. "He means a *piranha* fish."

Phil's face went very serious. "No, I'm talking about the Nyungani!"

"The *what*?" squeaked Chase.

"Look, I probably shouldn't tell you about—"

"No, no, tell me!" said Chase.

"Okay, well, the Nyungani is a red-eyed, hairy, man-like creature that lives in caves," said Phil.

"It has huge feet with pointed claws and razor sharp teeth," Michael added solemnly.

"Oh my God!" said Chase.

Before Chase could ask any more questions, Mrs Swift called out from the back door. "Time for bed boys! We've got another big day tomorrow so you need a good night's sleep."

But Chase hardly slept at all that night. All he could think about was the Nyungani.

The next day was another hot one, and Phil and Michael offered to take Fox, Chase, Lewis and Jimmy swimming.

"Don't worry," said Phil, "there are no crocodiles where we're going."

"Well, none that have been seen lately," said Michael.

They set off through the thick bush in single file, with Phil leading the way and Chase bringing up the rear. After 25 minutes of walking, Chase noticed his shoelace was undone and stopped to tie it up. It was one of those annoying shoelaces that always seemed to come undone no matter how tightly it was tied. Just as he finished tying a double knot, he spotted a stunning blue butterfly fluttering nearby and went over to take a closer look. It was the biggest butterfly Chase had ever seen, and he couldn't help but follow it for a few minutes as it danced its way between the trees. Suddenly Chase remembered that he was meant to be sticking with Michael and Phil, and rushed back to the spot where he had stopped to tie his shoelace.

Unfortunately, all the trees and bushes looked the same to Chase, and pretty soon he was completely lost. He thought about yelling out for help, but was scared that might attract a water buffalo, so he just kept walking.

Eventually he came to a clearing where there were giant rocks and a small waterfall. He stopped to catch his breath and try to work out what he was going to do. That's when he noticed a small cave just to the left of the waterfall. He looked a little closer and his heart almost stopped beating. Two red beady eyes were peering back at him from the darkness, and for a split second he caught a glimpse of a hairy creature with large feet and claws.

"It's a Ninja-Granny!" cried Chase.

He sprinted blindly through the bush, ignoring any scratches he received along the way.

A few minutes later he ran head first into Fox, nearly knocking him over.

"Chase! Where were you? We've been looking everywhere!"

Chase could hardly speak—partly because he was so scared and partly because he was so puffed out.

"You look like you've seen a ghost," said Phil.

"Worse!" said Chase, trying to catch his breath. "I ... saw ... a ... Ninja-Granny!"

"A Ninja-Gr ... you mean a Nyungani?" asked Michael.

"Yeah," said Chase, "one of those!"

Fox looked at his little brother. "Are you sure?" he asked doubtfully.

"I swear, Fox! It had red eyes, scary claws, it was all hairy—"

"Can you take us there?" interrupted Michael.

Chase looked at him for a moment and swallowed, then he nodded nervously and turned around, gesturing for them to follow him. Together they retraced the steps of his mad dash until they reached the clearing.

Chase pointed a slightly trembling hand towards the cave.

"It's in there," he said quietly.

They waited for nearly a minute and were about to give up, when suddenly a pair of red beady eyes appeared in the darkness.

"See, I told you—it's a Ninja-Granny!" cried Chase.

Fox held his breath as the monster slowly emerged from the cave. It was a wallaby!

Straight away Phil and Michael fell on the ground laughing, quickly followed by Fox and Lewis. Jimmy tried not to laugh because Chase was his best mate, but he couldn't resist and eventually burst out laughing too. Finally Chase joined in as well.

"Well hopefully that's the most embarrassing thing that will happen to me today," he said sheepishly.

"Come on," said Phil, "let's go for a swim."

Phil's special swimming spot was a little inlet only about 15 minutes from where Chase had spotted the "Nyungani".

On such a hot day the clear salt water was very refreshing. The boys were joking around and splashing each other when all of a sudden Chase felt a sharp pain in his right leg.

His first thought was that he'd been bitten by a crocodile, but when he looked down he saw a giant jellyfish had wrapped itself around his leg. He nearly fainted as the pain increased, but just managed to let out a feeble, "Help!"

Fox saw that Chase was in trouble and quickly swam over and dragged him out of the water. The jellyfish had disentangled itself, but Fox could see the giant red marks on Chase's leg where he had been stung.

Chase was trying to be brave, which wasn't easy, as he had never experienced pain like this. Fox tried to calm his brother down, but he had absolutely no idea how to help him.

That's when Michael and Phil took charge.

"Keep talking to him, Fox. Tell him to shut his eyes and he'll be okay."

Chase did as he was told, shutting his eyes and clenching his teeth, hoping the throbbing would go away.

All of a sudden he felt a small stream of liquid on his leg. Then another one. And another one. Whatever it was, it certainly soothed the pain and he started to relax.

That is, until Phil said, "It's always best to pee on a jellyfish sting."

Chase's eyes shot open.

"Only joking!" said Michael.

Chase was very relieved when he looked around and discovered the boys were squirting *sea*water, not *pee*-water on the sting.

"The look on your face when you thought they were peeing on you!" laughed Jimmy.

The sting was still very painful, but nowhere near as bad as it had been, and Chase managed a smile

"I'm not sure what's scarier—being attacked by a crocodile, seeing a Ninja-Granny, being stung by a giant jellyfish, or thinking you guys were peeing on me!"

Everyone burst out laughing.

"Definitely the last one," said Jimmy, and they all nodded in agreement.

That afternoon, while Chase was recovering in bed, Fox went to watch a local junior footy game between the Imalu Tigers and the Muluwurri Magpies.

Fox, who had taken his footy boots along so he could have a kick with Lewis and Jimmy at half-time, was amazed to discover that you didn't need footy boots to play on the Tiwi Islands. In fact only half the players were wearing them, and once the game started many of those players took off their boots and threw them over the boundary line.

TIWI PEE-WEE

It was a great game to watch. The local boys loved to run with the ball and they weaved in and out of congestion so gracefully it was as if they were moving in slow motion. Throughout the match players took spectacular marks and kicked some even more spectacular goals.

One thing was obvious from the very first bounce— the Tiwi kids had no fear. The Imalu Tigers kept throwing themselves into packs, but unfortunately more and more of their players suffered injuries. One kid rolled his ankle, two other players clashed heads, and another couple got crunched and winded in fierce tackles.

The game was really important to the Tigers, because a loss would mean they dropped out of the top four. At three-quarter time they trailed the Magpies by 19 points, and all the injuries meant they were facing the final quarter with just 17 fit players.

The coach of the Imalu Tigers, Mr Munkara, had seen Fox having a kick at half-time. He went over to him and said, "Would you like to sign up and play for the Tigers for a quarter?"

This was a dream come true for Fox, and he quickly filled out the form that Mr Munkara gave him. One of the injured players gave him his jumper, and Fox couldn't believe his luck when he saw that it had the No. 6 on the back. This was Fox's favourite number, and the one he wore when he played with the Diggers.

"That's got to be a good sign," he thought.

Mr Munkara told him to take up a position on the half-forward flank, and as Fox jogged onto the field he was desperate to play well for his new teammates.

He thought to himself, "Sure, you might not know how to handle water buffalo, crocodiles or jellyfish, but you do know how to play football. All you have to do is focus."

Suddenly Fox had his feet taken from under him. As he lay on the ground he could hear the crowd roaring with laughter. He looked up to see what had happened.

"Oh no, I've been bowled over by a pig!" he thought.

Sure enough, a wild pig had wandered onto the field and run straight through him.

Fox was totally embarrassed, and now more determined than ever to help the Tigers win. He didn't have to wait long for his first chance. When the Imalu rover shot out of the middle and kicked the footy long into the forward line, Fox swooped on the ball, baulked one Magpie player, blind turned around another, and calmly slotted a goal from 35 metres out.

The crowd went wild and Tigers players ran from everywhere to congratulate him.

Muluwurri quickly responded by kicking the next two goals, but the Tigers midfield answered the challenge and won the next four clearances. Each time the ball ended up in Fox's hands, and he kicked four more sensational goals.

The first was a freakish snap over his left shoulder; the second a torpedo punt from 40 metres out after taking a diving mark; the third was a grubber goal from the boundary; and the fourth came after dodging around four Magpie defenders.

The Tigers now trailed by three points. With 20 seconds to go, the ball was kicked high into the Imalu forward line. Fox ran back at full pace with the flight of the ball before twisting around at the last second and leaping high into the air. This ended with him sitting on the fullback's head and taking one of the bravest and most spectacular marks imaginable.

The second his feet landed on the ground in the right-hand forward pocket, the siren sounded. The umpire awarded Fox the mark and put him on **an acute angle**. It was a tricky kick and as the margin was three points, he needed to slot a goal for the Tigers to win. He weighed up his options—should he kick a drop punt with his left foot, or go with a banana kick on his right?

Fox held the ball on an angle that showed he was intending to take the banana option. He cleared his mind of any thoughts so he could focus entirely on what he needed to do, then he took a three-stride run-up and kicked. Everyone held their breath as the ball bent sharply to the right and flew straight over the goal umpire's head through the middle of the goals.

The crowd roared and all the Imalu players rushed over and lifted Fox onto their shoulders and carried him off the field. Even the pig that had knocked him over trotted back onto the ground and ran around to celebrate.

The Tigers players put Fox down as they crossed the boundary line and Mr Munkura rushed over.

"So Fox ... ever thought about moving to the Tiwi Islands?!" he asked.

TIWI PEE-WEE

On their last afternoon on the Tiwi Islands the Swifts and the Riolis went to an art gallery across the road from the Pularumpi school.

Several of the local artists working at the gallery were related to the Riolis, and Fox had a great chat to one of them in particular, a nice lady called Donna. He told her in great detail how much Cyril had helped the Diggers.

"Make sure you say hello to him for me next time you see him," said Donna.

"Sure thing," said Fox.

At this point more than 50 people from the islands had asked him to say hi to Cyril, so Fox decided it might be easier to just type out a list of all their names and email it to the Hawks star.

Mrs Swift bought a colourful painting of a sunrise and Mr Swift bought Imalu Tiger T-shirts for Fox and Chase.

As they left the gallery, Chase immediately put on his new T-shirt and handed his father the paper bag it had come in.

"Here's a gift for you, Dad," he said.

"What's that for?" asked Mr Swift.

"The flight back to Darwin!" said Chase.

"Very funny," said Mr Swift.

But he kept the bag, just in case.

6

Pumped Up for School

The first day of the school year always made Fox nervous.

That was because his father insisted on driving him and Chase, and always did something really embarrassing when they arrived. In the past he had sung a cheesy song, performed a dorky dance and last year he'd ended up in a drag race with Miles Winter.

But this year Fox had a plan. He set his alarm extra early and when it went off, he snuck quietly into Chase's room and woke him up.

The brothers showered and slipped into their school uniforms like mini ninjas, neither of them making a sound for fear of waking up their dad. When they were ready to go, they tiptoed out of the house and into the garage where their bikes were kept.

Fox smiled and whispered to Chase, "Dad will be so annoyed we outsmarted him this year!"

But when Fox went to hop on his bike, he immediately noticed a problem.

"Hey! My tyres are flat!"

"Mine too!" said Chase. "Front and back!"

"Don't panic," said Fox, "we just need to pump them up."

Unfortunately the pump wasn't in its usual place in the garage, and the boys couldn't find it anywhere. With their plan in ruins, they trudged back into the house, where they found their dad sitting in the kitchen sipping a cup of coffee.

"Morning!" he said cheerfully. "You guys are up early."

"Umm, Dad, have you seen the pump?" asked Fox.

"The pump?" said Mr Swift innocently. "Why do you need the pump?"

"Someone let down the tyres on our bikes," said Chase.

"Well, anyway, you guys won't be needing your bikes today," said Mr Swift. "I always drive you in on the first day—it's a tradition!"

"It's a tradition that you embarrass us," said Fox.

"Yeah, Dad, can you promise us you won't sing, dance or get into a drag race?" said Chase.

"Cross my heart and hope to die," said Mr Swift.

Despite his father's solemn promise, Fox wasn't 100 per cent convinced.

As soon as they jumped into the kombi, Fox immediately spotted the missing pump sticking out from underneath the front seat.

"Do you know anything about this, Dad?" he said, holding it up.

"No," said Mr Swift, trying to keep a straight face, "Your mother must have put it there."

Fox shook his head, and prayed that his dad wouldn't do anything to embarrass them when they arrived.

As soon as they pulled up in the school car park, the two boys bolted out of the kombi's side door and were about to rush off when Mr Swift called out to them.

"Hey, guys, hold up!"

"This is not good," whispered Fox.

Mr Swift jumped out of the kombi, pulled out his mobile phone, and said, "Let me take a first-day selfie."

Fox rolled his eyes, "Okay, Dad, but make it *really* quick."

"Yeah, quick, Dad, before anyone sees us," said Chase.

Mr Swift was about to take the photo when he spotted Miss Carey, the principal's quirky assistant.

"Hey, Miss Carey, would you like to be in a selfie?"

"Oh, Dad, please no," said Fox under his breath.

No one had ever asked Miss Carey to be in a selfie before, so she thought "Why not?" and went over to where Mr Swift and his two sons were standing.

"Well this can't get any worse," thought Fox.

He was wrong.

"Hey, Mr Percy, do you want to be in a selfie?" called out Mr Swift as the teacher walked by.

"Dad, nooooooo!" said Fox.

"Oooh a selfie!" said Mr Percy. "Don't mind if I do."

By now a large crowd of students had gathered to watch what was going on.

Mr Swift took the first selfie and the crowd gave a huge cheer. Fox hoped that the embarrassment was over, but again he was wrong.

"Okay, now let's take a few with different looks," said Mr Swift. "First up, I want everyone to show me a bit of attitude."

To Fox's amazement, Miss Carey and Mr Percy struck poses without hesitation. Miss Carey crossed her arms and put on an angry face, while Mr Percy flexed his non-existent muscles. Fox looked at Chase and wished there was a giant hole they could crawl into and hide.

The huge group of students who were looking on could not control their laughter.

Fox heard Lewis call out, "Work the camera, Mr P!"

Mr Percy did not need any encouragement. He pouted, raised his eyebrows and put his hands on his hips. When Mr Swift commanded everyone to look "cool", he even whipped out a pair of sunglasses.

"That one will be perfect for the first school newsletter of the year," said Mr Percy.

The thought of a photo of him and Chase with Mr Percy and Miss Carey being sent out to every kid at school sent a shiver up Fox's spine.

"Sorry, Dad, but we have to go to class—*now*," said Fox.

As he and Chase ran off, the crowd of about a hundred students gave a massive round of applause. Turning around for one last look, Fox saw his dad, Miss Carey and Mr Percy all taking a bow.

"He really outdid himself this year," said Fox, shaking his head.

"He is very, very good at being very, very bad," agreed Chase.

Fox was relieved to walk into his Year 8 classroom and see so many familiar faces. He went over to chat to Hugo and Chung, who were standing near the whiteboard.

"Bad news," said Hugo.

"What is it?" asked Fox.

"Mr Grinter is our teacher again."

"You're kidding!" moaned Fox.

"It could be worse," said Chung. "We could have had Rainbow Love!"

Something in the back corner of the classroom caught Fox's eye. Mace was talking to Vince, and he looked very unhappy with his dim-witted sidekick. Fox wondered what had happened.

The reason Mace was so unhappy was that he hadn't seen Vince all holidays. Vince's parents had sent him away to stay with his cousins because they thought Mace was a bad influence. After Vince was caught throwing eggs at the principal's house they decided the less their son saw of Mace the better.

Vince was very upset when his parents told him he would be spending the holidays at his aunt and uncle's house. His uncle was some sort of important professor, and his cousins were real nerds who were always doing scientific experiments.

What surprised Vince was that he ended up having the best holiday of his life. He was amazed at how much he enjoyed hanging out with his cousins. They taught him how to do a whole lot of really cool experiments, and he taught them how to kick a footy. He wished he could have stayed longer with his relatives, but he could never admit this to Mace.

"How was it staying with your loser cousins?" sneered Mace.

"Oh, it was gr—I mean, awful. Like, the worst summer ever," said Vince.

"Well you missed out big time! Dad bought a brand new quad motorbike, and it's so cool to ride."

Mace looked down at the desk and noticed a glasses case. "What's that?"

Vince nervously opened the case and put on a pair of thick glasses with big black frames.

"Nerd alert!" yelled Mace.

"Shhh!" said Vince. "I wasn't able to see the whiteboard very well, and my mum thinks that might be why I've been getting such bad marks at school."

"As if!" scoffed Mace. "The reason you get bad marks is because you're *thick*!"

He then pulled a brand new mobile phone out of his pocket and waved it in front of Vince's face.

"But here's something that *isn't* thick—look how skinny it is!"

"Be careful, Mace," said Vince, looking around nervously. "We're not allowed to have mobiles at school."

Chung had seen Mace holding up his phone and came over.

"Hey, Mace. Cool phone. Can I have a look?"

"No way! I don't want to get Chung germs!" said Mace.

Chung simply smiled and said, "No worries, Mace. Have a nice day."

Mace watched Chung suspiciously as he walked off, but was quickly distracted when he saw that their class had a new student.

"Come with me, Vince," he said, "let's welcome the newbie."

Mace walked over to the new kid and tapped him on the shoulder. The boy had dark hair, light brown skin and a warm smile.

"What's ya name?" grunted Mace

"Aslam—"

"Pfffft! What sort of a weirdo name is that? Where ya from?"

"Iran—"

"Well you're not welcome here, so why don't you go back to Iraq—"

"Um, Mace he said he was from *Iran*," said Vince.

"Iraq, Iran—it's all the same!" snapped Mace.

"Actually, Mace, I'm pretty sure Iraq is spelt with a 'Q'," said Vince thoughtfully.

"Shut up, Vince!"

Fox walked over with Lewis and Simon to introduce himself to the new guy and make sure he was okay.

"Hi, I'm Fox, and this is Lewis and Simon," he said.

"Hi, I'm Aslam Khan," said the new boy.

"If Mace was being mean to you it's not his fault," said Lewis. "He has a serious medical condition—he was born without a heart."

"You never told me that, Mace!" said Vince.

"Shut up, Vince!"

"Hey, Aslam, if you want to have a kick of the footy at recess, come and join us on the oval," suggested Fox.

Aslam's eyes lit up, "Thanks, Fox, that'd be cool."

"Ha!" sneered Mace. "He's probably a Muslim—and as if Muslims can play footy!"

"What about Bachar Houli, Mace?"

"Shut up, Vince!"

At this point Mr Grinter walked in and everyone rushed to sit down.

As usual, the curly red-headed teacher was more than 10 minutes late. His fashion sense clearly hadn't improved over the holidays either—he was wearing brown corduroy pants with a shiny plastic grey belt, black shoes and a short-sleeved lime-green shirt. He already had two enormous sweat stains under his arms, and Fox wondered if these would join up by lunchtime. Mr Grinter was also wearing a purple bow tie, because he thought it made him look more intelligent. As it turned out, he was the only one that thought that.

"Sorry I'm late—there were, um, sheep on the road," he said, remembering an article he'd read in the newspaper a while ago.

Mr Grinter glanced over at Sally Renton in the front row. He was expecting to see her scribbling down a nasty note about him for her father, the school's principal, but for once she wasn't writing—she was typing.

"Is that an iPad, Sally?" he asked nervously.

Sally folded her arms and nodded.

Mr Grinter frowned, "Unfortunately, no personal electronic equipment is allowed in the classroom. That includes smart phones, iPods, iPads and—"

"Tumble driers!" called out Lewis.

"And tumble driers," repeated Mr Grinter without thinking. "No, not tumble driers—"

"So you're saying we *can* use tumble driers in class?" said Lewis.

"No, you can *not* use tumble driers in class!" said Mr Grinter.

"And you definitely can't use smartphones or tablets," he said, returning his gaze to Sally. "Is that rule clear to everyone?"

"Yes, Mr Grinter," groaned the class.

Sally scowled and powered down her iPad, and Mr Grinter looked quite smug—until he saw Sally pull out a piece of paper and start scribbling furiously.

Fox noted that his teacher's underarm sweat stains had now officially joined up. It almost looked like he had fallen into a puddle.

"Okay, now that everyone knows the rules—" said Mr Grinter.

But before he could finish his sentence, he was interrupted by Mace's mobile phone going off. It had a *Bob the Builder* ringtone.

While the rest of the class erupted with laughter, Mace glared at Chung, who was trying to look as innocent as possible.

7

Laser Show

At recess most of the kids from Fox's class headed out for a kick of the footy.

Mace, Vince and a couple of their Dragons teammates made their way to one end of the school oval, and Fox and his Diggers friends went to the other.

"Do you want come up this end, Aslam?" asked Fox.

"No, I might try my luck over here," said the new kid, trotting down to stand near Mace.

Fox was surprised, but Mace was delighted.

"This guy's name is Khan," he said, turning to Vince. "That's short for *Khan* hardly play!"

"Really? That's a pretty long surname. No wonder he shortened it."

"Shut up, Vince! Let's give this kid a football lesson."

The ball was kicked up to where Mace and Vince were standing and they both flew for the ball and **spoiled each other**.

Before the ball could hit the ground Aslam sprinted through like a steam train and **gathered possession**.

Fox instinctively led out and Aslam delivered a 35-metre right-foot drop-punt pass with pinpoint accuracy straight to the Diggers captain's outstretched hands.

"Brilliant pass!" said Fox with a huge smile on his face.

"You must have a laser in dem shoes!" said Lewis in an American accent.

From that moment, Aslam became known as 'Laser' Khan.

"You idiot, Vince! Why did you spoil me?" cried Mace. "Stop making that loser look good!"

Fox kicked the footy up the other end again and this time Vince marked it unopposed. A split second after he took the ball, Aslam ran by calling, "Vince, Vince, Vince!"

Vince heard his name and automatically handballed to Aslam, who this time delivered a low-trajectory **worm burner** pass to the leading Simon Phillips. This time the kick was with his left foot.

"Top kick again, Laser!" called out Fox.

Mace was furious.

"Vince! Why did you handball it to him? This time let's wait until he gets the ball and then we'll crunch him."

"Gotcha, Mace. *Khan* see him getting out of this one," said Vince with a grin.

"Stop stealing my jokes!" snapped Mace.

When the footy next came their way, Mace and Vince deliberately stood at the front of the pack and waited for Aslam to come charging through. Sure enough, the ball spilt off three sets of hands and was plucked out of the air by the new kid, who had timed his run to perfection. All of a sudden Mace and Vince appeared in front of him and dived at him just as he was about to kick the ball.

Fox watched as Laser somehow pulled the ball back up to his waist just before kicking it. He stopped on the spot and sidestepped to his left before shooting off again, causing Mace and Vince to crash into each other as he flashed past them.

"That's what I call **selling candy**!" yelled out Lewis.

As Mace and Vince lay on the ground rubbing their heads, Aslam kicked a perfect pass to Bruno Gallucci, the centre half-back for the Diggers.

"Hey, Bruno," said Fox, "how would you like to have Laser linking up with you and Mo in the backline?"

"That would be *awesome!*" replied Bruno.

As they walked back to class, Fox asked Laser where he had learned to play such brilliant footy. Aslam explained that he had watched two guards kicking a footy to each other while he and his family were living in a detention centre near Sydney. It was just after they had arrived in Australia, and he'd fallen in love with Aussie Rules on the spot.

Aslam had been very excited to discover there was an AFL player called Bachar Houli who was Muslim, just like his family. He had written the Richmond star a letter, and Bachar had been so impressed that the next time he was in Sydney he went to visit Aslam. He even gave him a brand-new footy with the signatures of all his Richmond teammates on it! From that day on Aslam had been a passionate Tigers fan, and kept a scrapbook full of newspaper cuttings about the team.

"The Diggers have a yellow sash just like the Tigers so you'll feel right at home playing for us," said Fox when he heard this.

When the students arrived back at the classroom, Mr Grinter told them that the principal wanted to make an important announcement and they all had to go to the assembly hall.

As they sat waiting for Mr Renton, Fox watched a bird fly back and forth across the ceiling. He was always on high alert whenever a bird accidentally found its way into the assembly hall, as he was worried it might drop a little unwelcome present on some poor kid's head. But his birdwatching was soon interrupted by Mr Renton sweeping in from the back of the hall with all the other teachers trailing after him. The students stood up and waited for Mr Renton to arrive at the lectern on the stage at the front of the hall.

"You may sit down," he said in his serious principal's voice.

"Welcome everyone. I have a very big announcement to start off the term. This year, for the first time in our school's history, we are going to elect a school captain.

There was an excited murmur among the students and Mr Renton held up his hand to quieten everyone down. The principal had not considered a school captain was necessary until the day before, when he'd had to fill out a survey from the Department of Education. There was a section called "Developing Leadership", which awarded an extra 10 points to schools that had a school captain.

"Because electing a school captain is a brand-new concept, I will explain the rules," he said. "The first rule is that a candidate must be nominated by a student other than himself or herself. The second rule is that a third student must then second the nomination. Please remember that you may only nominate or second a nomination for *one* student. If there is more than one person nominated for school captain, then there will be a vote held by secret ballot at lunchtime. Is that clear?"

Most of the students looked confused, but Mr Renton pushed ahead anyway.

"So are there any nominations?"

After a short pause, Lewis yelled out, "Yes, I nominate Fox Swift!"

CAPTAIN SWIFT

Fox looked at his best mate in shock as most of the kids in the hall gave a thunderous round of applause.

Mace folded his arms and sat there stewing jealously as the clapping continued. He elbowed Vince in the stomach and out of the side of his mouth said, "You know what to do!"

"Huh?" said Vince

"Do it!"

"Are you sure, Mace?

"Yes of course I'm sure!"

"Really?"

"Yes!"

"Now?"

"Yes now!"

"Okay ..." said Vince a little uncertainly, before clearing his throat and calling out, "I *second* Fox Swift!"

"What?! You idiot, Vince!" hissed Mace. "You were supposed to nominate me!"

"Thank you, Vincent," said Mr Renton. "We now have a nomination and a second for Fox Swift. Are there any other nominations?"

Mace grabbed a third-grader sitting in front of him roughly by the shoulder and whispered menacingly, "Nominate me or you die!"

Mr Renton spotted the little kid's trembling hand go up and heard his squeaky voice call out, "I nominate— um, what's your name again?"

Everyone burst out laughing.

"Mace Winter! It's Mace Winter, you little twerp!"

"Oh yeah, Mace Winter."

"Okay, do I have a seconder for Mace?" asked Mr Renton.

There was an awkward silence. "Vince!" hissed Mace as he elbowed his mate in the stomach once again.

"Oh, right," said Vince. "I second Mace Winter."

But Mr Renton shook his head.

"I'm sorry, Vincent, but you are only allowed to second one candidate, and you've already seconded Fox Swift."

"Oops!" said Vince, trying to ignore Mace's death stare.

"So does anyone else want to second Mace Winter's nomination?" asked Mr Renton.

The hall immediately went so quiet you could hear the cicadas chirping outside.

"So, with Fox Swift being the only nomination with a seconder, I declare him to be our school's first ever captain."

Fox went bright red as all the students rose and gave him a standing ovation. Well, all the students apart from Mace. Even Vince stood up and started clapping, although he was quickly dragged back down into his seat.

Mace was ready to explode with rage. "This is definitely the worst moment of my life," he thought.

As if on cue, the bird that had been flying around the hall chose that exact moment to drop a squishy dollop of poo—straight onto Mace's head.

"No, I was wrong—*this* is the worst moment of my life," he thought as the white gloop ran down the side of his face.

LASER SHOW

Mr Renton asked Fox to come to his office after school to collect his school captain certificate.

So that afternoon when the bell rang Fox made his way over to the school administration building and into the waiting room outside the principal's office. The room appeared to be deserted—but Fox knew from experience that looks could be deceiving. He scanned the walls and the ceiling, and even looked behind the large pot plant in the corner to make sure he was really alone. All of a sudden he heard a knocking sound.

Force of habit made him say, "Come in!" and Miss Carey's head popped up above her desk. She was holding a tiny hammer and wearing a stethoscope, like the one his doctor used to listen to his heartbeat.

"Termites," she said, as if that explained everything.

Then, dropping back down to her hands and knees, she held her stethoscope up to the wooden skirting board and continued tapping it with the hammer.

When Mr Renton came into the room to invite Fox into his office and saw his secretary listening to the wall's heartbeat, he didn't know what to say.

He looked at Fox for an explanation, but Fox merely shrugged his shoulders and said, "Termites."

"That's right," said Miss Carey as she continued to tap away. "One termite can bring down an entire building!"

Five minutes later, as Fox was leaving the principal's office, he noticed that Miss Carey had removed part of the skirting board and was chipping away at the brick with a tiny chisel.

She appeared to be talking to the wall, and Fox was pretty sure he heard her mutter, "I've got you now."

At dinner that night, Fox was asked a lot of questions by his parents about being school captain. He was very keen to change the subject, so he asked Chase about his day.

"It was a disaster!" said his younger brother. "D-E-S-A-S-T-E-R, disaster."

"Did this disaster involve a spelling test?" asked Mr Swift, trying not to smile.

"Huh?" said Chase.

"What your father means is why was it such a bad day?" said Mrs Swift.

"You'll never guess who my teacher is—Rainbow Love! And she just L-U-V-S, *loves* the Winter twins."

"Maybe that's because they're good at spelling?" said Mr Swift.

"At least you don't have Mr Percy this year," said Fox, trying to cheer up his brother.

"That's true," said Chase. "Fingers crossed I won't have to speak to him all year."

"Yeah," said Fox, "that would be a total D-E-S-A-S-T-E-R."

Chase had no idea why everyone except him thought this was so amusing.

8

'D' Day

"You are the smartest person in the world," said Miles Winter.

He was looking at his reflection in the bathroom mirror at the time. His wife, who was cleaning her teeth next to him, shook her head.

"If you're so smart," she said, "how come you forgot to put the bins out last night?"

Miles ignored this snide remark and went back to thinking about his superior intelligence.

The year before, the junior football league had kicked the Dragons out of the competition for paying their players. But after going through the rulebook, Miles had discovered there was nothing in there to stop him from simply re-registering the club under a different name.

So the day after the humiliating Grand Final, he had gone to the junior football league's website and printed off a list of all the names that were available for new clubs. The list was in alphabetical order, which made things very easy for Miles, who was specifically interested in the ones that started with the letter 'D'. Among those, there was one in particular that stood out.

"Dragonflies!" he said to himself. "It's too perfect—the Davinal Dragonflies."

He figured the team could immediately start calling themselves the Dragons for short. Everything would be back to the way it was, and there was nothing the league could do to stop them.

"You really are a genius," said Miles into the mirror as he applied some underarm spray.

"Hey, genius," said his wife, "that's shaving cream, not deodorant."

Miles wiped away the white foamy evidence of his stupidity and stormed out of the bathroom.

Applications to register new teams were closing at midday that day and Miles had arranged to meet the president of the junior football league, Mabel 'Hannibal' Hurley, at 11.45am. All he had to

A close shave?

do was pay the registration fee and let Mabel know that the name of the new team was the Dragonflies.

Miles let Mace and Vince tag along with him, and was in such a good mood he even bought them both an ice cream before the meeting.

"Single cone, one scoop only," he reminded them.

While they were eating their ice creams, Miles' mobile phone rang. It was a reporter from the *Davinal Digest* who wanted to interview him about the importance of family values.

"It would be great if we could take a photo of you with one of your sons as part of the story," said the reporter.

"Oooh a photo! Yes, that sounds great," said Miles. "I have a meeting in 15 minutes, so could we do the interview later on this afternoon?"

"Sorry, Miles, this afternoon's no good," said the reporter. "Our photographer has to leave to do a job in Romana in half an hour. I'll give Jack Swift a call and see if he wants to do the interview—"

"Wait!" screamed Miles down the phone. "I'll do it! I'll do it! I'll be there with my son Mace in 15 minutes."

Miles hung up and took a deep breath. He was about to do something he never wanted to do—rely on Vince.

"Vince, I need you to do me a favour," he said.

"No problemo, Mr W," said Vince.

Miles winced. He hated it when Vince called him Mr W.

'D' DAY

"Mace and I have to do an important newspaper interview," he said. "So I need you to take this cheque to Mrs Hurley, and tell her our new team will be called the Dragonflies. Have you got that?"

"No problemo, Mr W," said Vince.

"So what's the name of the new team?" asked Miles.

"Umm, it's the ... umm ..."

Miles put his head in his hands. "It's the Dragonflies, okay? The Dragonflies!"

"Got it!" said Vince.

"So what is it?" asked Mace.

"It's the ... Flydragons?" said Vince hopefully.

"No, it's the Dragonflies!" yelled Miles.

"Hey, it's not my fault," said Vince. "I'm no good with names—I'm only good with numbers."

"Okay then, I've got an idea," said Miles, looking at the list of all the available names starting with 'D'.

- Darts
- Deers
- Devils
- Dingoes
- Dolphins
- Doves
- Dragonflies
- Drongos
- Drovers
- Ducks
- Dynamos

"Vince, the name we want is fifth from the bottom on this list. Can you remember that?" said Mr Winter.

"Yep, fifth from the bottom. Got it." said Vince. "See, I'm good with numbers!"

"Mmm, well Mace and I have to go. Here's the cheque and the list. Remember it's—"

"Fifth from the bottom."

"Excellent!" said Miles as he sped off with Mace to do the *Davinal Digest* interview.

Vince put the cheque in his top pocket for safekeeping and put the list of names in the pocket of his tracksuit pants.

Vince walked confidently into Mrs Hurley's office and sat down in a chair on the other side of her desk. Mabel 'Hannibal' Hurley wasn't happy about the Dragons being able to re-register under a different name, but she was bound by the rules of the competition.

"Hi Mrs Hannibal—"

"It's Mrs Hurley."

"Ooh sorry—Mrs Hurley. Mr Winter couldn't make it, so he sent me along to register the new team."

Vince pulled out the cheque from his top pocket and handed it to Mabel.

"This seems to be in order," said Mabel, inspecting the cheque, "so what's the new name you'd like to register?"

"I've got the list right here," said Vince.

He had just reached into the pocket of his tracksuit paints when he suddenly realised he didn't actually *have* a pocket in his tracksuit pants! He had merely slipped the list down the side of his pants, and it must have fallen out in the street somewhere.

"Uh oh, I've lost the list!" he said.

"What list?" asked Mabel.

"The one with all the 'D' names available. It was the fifth name from the bottom," said Vince.

"Don't worry," said Mabel, "I can look that up on line."

She quickly tapped away on the keyboard, and in less than five seconds the list was on the screen in front of her. It had been recently updated and a new name, the Dumptrucks, had been added. Mabel counted up five from the bottom, and smiled.

"Are you *sure* you want to register the name that's fifth from the bottom?" she asked.

"Definitely," said Vince. "I'm very good with numbers."

Mr Winter was in a filthy mood when he and Mace caught up with Vince 45 minutes later.

"How was the interview, Mr W?" asked Vince.

"Terrible. That stupid reporter kept asking questions that made me look bad."

"Like what?"

"Ridiculous questions like, 'What is the date of your wife's birthday?' I mean, how am I supposed to know that?"

"It's the 17th of May," said Vince.

Miles stared at Vince. "How do you know that?" he asked.

Vince shrugged his shoulders and said, "I'm good with numbers."

"So, how did you go with Mrs Hurley?" said Miles, changing the subject.

"Great!" said Vince. "Here's your receipt and the vegetation papers—"

Mr Winter snatched the pieces of paper from Vince.

"It's *registration* papers, you clot! Let's see now," he said as he flicked through the paperwork. When he saw the new name of the footy team, his face went bright red and he let out a noise that sounded like a cat coughing up a furball.

"No, it can't be! Vince, what did you do?"

"Nothing, Mr W!" said Vince. "I said the fifth name from the bottom, just like you told me to."

Mabel had attached the updated list of 'D' names to the registration papers, and sure enough Dragonflies was no longer fifth last.

"Let's not panic," said Mr Winter, panicking. "I'll call Mabel and sort it out with her."

Miles pulled out his phone and quickly punched in Mrs Hurley's phone number.

"Hi Mabel, how are you going? Beautiful day today, isn't—"

"What do you want, Miles?" said Mabel, cutting him off.

"Um, I think there has been a teensy little mistake with the vegetation ... I mean registration papers, and I just wanted to—"

"What mistake is that, Miles?" Mabel asked innocently.

"Well, the name we *meant* to register was the Dragonflies, so if you could just pull out some correction fluid at your end and make the change—"

"Sorry, Miles, the registration period closed half an hour ago, so there's nothing I can do. Those are the rules."

"But ... but ... you can't do that!"

"Your team either plays under the name Vince registered, or they don't play at all," said Mabel sternly before hanging up.

All Miles could do was stand there holding his phone and shaking his head in disbelief.

"What is it, Dad?" asked Mace. "What's our new name?"

Miles handed his son the list of names and said, "Fifth name from the bottom."

- Darts
- Deers
- Devils
- Dingoes
- Dolphins
- Doves
- Dragonflies
- Drongos
- Drovers
- Ducks
- Dumptrucks
- Dynamos

"The **Drongos**?" said Mace. "What's a drongo?"

"It means idiot, you idiots!" screamed Miles.

"Look on the bright side, Mace," said Vince. "You'll always be known as the original captain of the Drongos."

"Shut up, Vince!" said Miles and Mace together.

One that got away

9

A Winter's Roast

Fox knew how hard it was to deal with one Winter in the classroom, and he felt very sorry for his younger brother, who had to put up with two of them.

So Fox wasn't too surprised when Chase came up to him at recess one morning and said, "As school captain, are you allowed to throw people into the school dungeon?"

"No—and I'm pretty sure the school doesn't have a dungeon," said Fox. "How come?"

"Magnus and Murdoch Winter, that's how come."

"What have they done now?" asked Fox.

"They said that because the Diggers don't have an under-11s team, Jimmy and I are going to have to play for the Drongos."

Fox knew what he would do if he was in Chase's shoes, but he always let his younger brother come up with his own solutions.

"So what are you going to do about it?" he asked.

"Jimmy and I are going to start our own under-11s team at the Diggers."

Fox smiled. He was very proud of Chase, but of course he didn't want him to know that, so he just said, "Mmm, not a bad idea."

"I've organised for a few kids to come around to our place for a training session after school," said Chase, "and Jimmy and I were hoping you and some of the older Diggers players could help us out."

"No worries," said Fox. "Anything to stop you from being a Drongo."

Fox asked Hugo and Lewis to assist the young Diggers recruits that afternoon, and they both happily agreed.

While they waited for Chase and Jimmy's mates to arrive, Fox explained what he wanted his friends to do.

"Hugo, how about you run the drills?"

Hugo was surprised that Fox had asked him to take on such an important role.

"Shouldn't you do that?" he asked.

"No, you are much better at explaining how to do things," said Fox. "You're a natural coach. Just keep it simple and these guys will learn a lot."

Hugo was pretty chuffed to have received such a compliment from the best junior footballer he had seen.

"Sure thing," he said.

"And what about me?" said Lewis. "Or am I just here just for my good looks?"

"You keep telling yourself that, Lewis," said Fox with a smile. "What I really want you to do is make sure they all have fun. That's probably the most important thing, especially for kids who haven't played much before."

Lewis put on the most boring voice he could and, sounding exactly like Mr Grinter, said, "Okay. Fox. I. Will. Try. To. Be. Funny."

Fox cracked up. Even when Lewis was trying not to be funny, he was hilarious.

The sound of the front doorbell carried through to the backyard.

"I'll get it!" yelled Chase as he and Jimmy sprinted up the hallway.

A minute later they reappeared through the back sliding door with the biggest 10-year-old Fox had ever seen.

"Wow!" said Lewis. "That guy just blocked out the sun."

Fox estimated that the boy was almost as tall as his two mates Sammy and Chris, but he had an especially massive head, a barrel chest and his legs were the size of tree trunks.

"Hugo, I think the under-11s might have found a ruckman," said Fox, grinning from ear to ear.

Chase brought over his giant friend and said, "Fox, Lewis and Hugo, this is Gregor Ivanisovich."

Gregor smiled and let out a huge burp.

"I hereby christen you 'The Burpinator'," said Lewis.

The next classmate to arrive was a girl named Masumi Kato, whose family had moved over from Japan when she was a baby.

After being introduced, Hugo asked her if she had

much experience kicking a footy. Masumi walked over to a ball that was lying on the ground nearby, rolled it towards herself with her foot, flicked it up in the air, grabbed it and speared a perfect drop-punt pass to Jimmy, who was standing 25 metres away.

"Okay, so you probably don't need me to teach you how to kick," said Hugo sheepishly.

At that moment a tall, dark-haired, laidback-looking kid wearing sunglasses and listening to an iPod strolled into the Swift's backyard.

"Hey Zeb," said Chase. "What are you listening to?"

"Courtney Barnett," said the boy.

"Cool," said Chase, nodding his head enthusiastically.

"Who's Courtney Barnett?" Fox whispered to his brother.

"I don't have a clue," Chase whispered back. "But if this guy is listening to her, she must be really cool."

Chase introduced the boy to the older Diggers as Zebidiah Fontaine.

"He's even got a really cool name," thought Fox.

Fox immediately recognised Chase and Jimmy's next two recruits, Minoo Saaed (Sammy's younger sister) and Subin Wek (Chris' younger sister). They were both built exactly like their brothers: tall and athletic.

Lewis started calling Minoo 'Mini', which was

funny given how tall she was, and all the kids called Subin 'Soobs'.

The last person to arrive was a tall boy named Adesh Gupta. His family had also come from another country, India, when he was five years old. Adesh had the longest arms Fox had ever seen, and straight away Lewis started calling him 'Inspector Gadget'.

"Are there any more coming, Chase?" asked Fox.

"No. The only one who couldn't make it was 'JT', but he's really keen to be a Digger."

Fox had seen JT around the school. His real name was Johnny Ticker, and he stood out because he had lost most of his left arm in a car accident when he was very young. Fox looked forward to meeting him because according to Chase he was "the best bloke ever".

The backyard training session was a huge success. Hugo did a fantastic job with the drills and Lewis did just as well with keeping things fun. In fact the group had such a good time, they all said they wanted to play together in a new Davinal Diggers under-11s team.

At the dinner table that night Chase asked his brother what he thought their chances were of fielding a decent team.

Mr and Mrs Swift rolled their eyes as if to say, "Here we go."

"The boys talking about footy at the dinner table—

who would have thought?" said Mr Swift sarcastically.

Fox ignored his parents and said to his brother, "You are going to have an amazing team."

"Really?" said Chase unable to hide his relief.

"Starting with Gregor: if he doesn't get reported for burping, he will be unbeatable in the ruck. Masumi is like Paige, deadly on either foot. I'm telling you now she will kick a load of goals. Mini has the most amazing leap—she will take 'mark of the day' every week. Soobs is lightning fast and can run all day. Zeb Fontaine, or 'The Zedman' as Lewis calls him, is the smoothest young player I have ever seen. He looks like he's not trying, but he is a dead-set star. And Adesh will dominate at full-back with those long arms of his—no one is ever going to out-mark him. Throw in you and Jimmy on the ball, and you have a very talented core of a footy team. "

Chase nodded thoughtfully. "Are we missing any key position players?"

"Maybe a centre half-back. It would help out Adesh if you had another strong defender, but you have so many star players you'll do well anyway."

Mr and Mrs Swift watched their sons have this in-depth and very serious conversation about the strengths and weaknesses of a yet to be assembled football team.

"If only they could apply that amount of thought and concentration to a topic like world peace," sighed Mrs Swift.

At school the next morning the Winter twins were once again teasing Chase and Jimmy about having to play with the Drongos. And as if being bullies wasn't bad enough, Murdoch and Magnus also had a really annoying habit of finishing each other's sentences.

Murdoch snarled, "You losers will never be able to—"

"—have your own team," said Magnus.

"You know how I know you guys are identical?" said Jimmy with a smile. "Because I can't tell which one of you is more annoying."

Chase laughed and said, "And for your information

we will have our own Diggers team—and it's going to be a really good team, too!"

"Sure it will," scoffed Murdoch.

"Yeah, who's going to play for the stupid Diggers?" said Magnus.

"Oh, I don't know—how about Jimmy, me, Gregor, Masumi, Zeb, Mini, Soobs, Adesh and JT for starters?" said Chase.

"JT?!" said Murdoch. "As if he can play!"

"Yeah, he'd be hopeless," laughed Magnus. "He's only got one arm!"

Chase took a step forward. The fierce look in his eye made the twins take two steps backwards.

"Anyone should be allowed to play footy—it doesn't matter who you are or whether you have a disability or not. I've never seen JT play—he could be a star for all I know, but who cares? As long as he wants to play, that's all that matters."

Chase took another step forward and the twins now had their backs pressed up against the wall.

"And I don't care if there are two of you—if you ever say another thing about JT, I'm going make you regret it."

Unfortunately Chase hadn't noticed his teacher Rainbow Love entering the classroom. The only part of the conversation she heard was him saying, "I'm going to make you regret it."

"Chase Swift!" she said, sounding shocked. "Violence is never a solution."

She looked at Murdoch and Magnus. "Are you two okay?"

"A bit shaken," said Murdoch.

"Yeah, we were just minding our own business and Chase lost it," said Magnus.

Chase and Jimmy tried to explain their side of the story but Ms Love cut them off.

"Uh, uh—I heard what you said, Chase, and there is no excuse for that aggressive behaviour," she said.

While Ms Love was focusing her attention on Chase, the twins started pulling faces at him behind her back. This made him even angrier.

"Chase, you will apologise to Magnus and Murdoch in front of the class immediately," said Ms Love. "And if you don't, you will have a detention after school!"

When Chase arrived home after his detention that evening, he knew his parents would be unhappy. And he knew they would be really unhappy after he handed them the letter Ms Love had sent home with him.

A WINTER'S ROAST

Dear Mr and Mrs Swift,

It brings me no joy to have to tell you that I caught Chase picking on two of his classmates today.

Murdoch and Magnus Winter are such sensitive souls, and they were deeply upset by Chase's threatening behaviour. I was particularly disappointed that Chase refused to apologise to the innocent parties.

I suggest you send Chase to his room so that he knows he has done the wrong thing. I will be checking in with him in the morning to see what punishment you gave him.

Yours faithfully,
Ms Rainbow Love

Mr Swift read the letter and looked at Chase.

"How about you go off to your room to think about what happened today? Your mother and I will be there shortly," he said.

Chase shook his head and slowly walked to his bedroom.

What he didn't know was that his parents knew the true story about his fight with the twins after Jimmy had told Lewis, who had told Fox, who had told them.

Chase was on his bed staring at the ceiling and feeling

pretty down when he thought he smelled something. Something good. His door burst open and in walked Fox and his parents carrying trays with plates piled high with food.

"A roast!" said Chase in surprise.

"Your favourite!" said Mr Swift.

"And we have chocolate ripple cake for dessert," said Mrs Swift.

"My other favourite!" said Chase.

Fox could tell his brother was confused, especially when Chase said, "Um, what's going on?"

"If your teacher asks you about your punishment," said Mrs Swift, "tell her we sent you to your room and didn't let you out all night."

"More gravy, Chase?" asked Mr Swift with a smile.

10

A Chocolate Surprise

Chase had never felt so nervous about making a phone call.

Fox watched his brother take a deep breath before picking up the receiver and slowly pushing the buttons. After six rings Chase was about to hang up when he heard a familiar voice.

"Hello, Greg Scott speaking."

Chase wanted to ask Mr Scott a big favour, but he wasn't quite sure where to start.

"Um, hi Mr Scott, it's Chase here, um, Chase Swift, and I was, like, just wondering if you would, and hey I totally understand if you don't want to because I know you're really busy—"

Fox rolled his eyes and made circles in the air with his hand as a signal for Chase to hurry up and get to the point.

Chase took another deep breath and blurted out, "Jimmy and I are starting up a Diggers under-11s team and we were hoping you could be our coach."

"No worries, Chase," said Mr Scott. "You and Jimmy helped me out last year when we were short of players. I'd love to coach you guys."

Fox could tell by the look on his brother's face that the news was good. He knew Mr Scott would say yes because he loved coaching so much. The Diggers under-11s would be playing immediately before the under-14s, so it would just mean Mr Scott would need to arrive at the ground a few hours earlier.

Chase hung up the phone.

"Yesssss! I can't wait for school tomorrow," he said.

"How come?" asked Fox

"To see the look on Magnus' and Murdoch's faces!"

"Dad, we need to talk," said Magnus.

Miles was shocked. The Winter family rarely spoke to each other at the dinner table, as they were usually too busy playing with their smartphones or iPads.

"What is it? You two haven't been playing with matches again?"

"Of course not," said Murdoch. This wasn't strictly true, but the twins wanted to talk about a far more important issue.

"It's Chase Swift—did you know he's trying to start up an under-11s Diggers team?"

"Ha, he has no chance," said Miles.

"Well he's doing it—and they might have some really good players," said Magnus.

"And now they've got Mr Scott, so they'll have the best coach," added Murdoch.

"Well, not the *best* coach—" said Mr Winter.

Miles expected his sons to say, "Apart from *you*, Dad!" and was quite disappointed when they stared at him blankly.

"Well I'll put a stop to that," said Miles. "Mercedes, hand me my phone."

"You're already holding it, you goose," said Mrs Winter.

"Oh, so I am," said Mr Winter, and he started punching numbers into his phone.

"Hello, Mabel Hurley speaking," said the voice on the other end of the line.

"Oh, hi Mabel, it's Miles Winter here—"

"Well I'm kind of in the middle of dinner at the moment—"

"This won't take long and it's *very* important."

Miles ignored Mabel's rather loud sigh and continued talking.

"As you know, I made a small mistake last year about the rules of the competition—"

"A *small* mistake! You secretly paid junior footballers—"

"My point is, I hear another club is about to breach the rules and I don't want them to get into trouble."

"What is it, Miles?"

"I'm just doing it for the children—"

"What is it Miles?!" snapped Mabel.

"The league rules clearly state that a person can only coach one side at their club, and unfortunately it looks like Greg Scott is planning to coach the Diggers under-11s *and* under-14s."

Mabel Hurley rolled her eyes. Miles was actually correct, but she was well aware his motives weren't as honourable as he made out.

"Thanks for bringing this to my attention, Miles. I'll let Mr Scott know he can only coach the one side."

"Thanks Mabel. As you know I'm just doing this for the childr—hello? Mabel? Hmm, we must have been cut off."

Fox looked on as Chase and Jimmy counted out all their pocket money.

"That makes $7.50," said Jimmy. "Do you think this will work?"

"Can you think of a better way to find a coach?"

A CHOCOLATE SURPRISE

Jimmy shook his head. Chase put all their coins into a large jar, and he and Jimmy rode their bikes to the *Davinal Digest*'s office.

They were greeted at the counter by the newspaper's owner, Andy Watson. Mr Watson was a very friendly man who knew everyone in town, and everyone knew him.

"What can I do for you, boys?" he said with a smile.

"We'd like to place an ad in your paper, Mr Watson," said Jimmy.

"Really? What sort of an ad?"

"Well, you see, we're starting up our own footy team, the Davinal Diggers under-11s," said Chase. "And we were going to get Mr Scott, who coaches the under-14s team, to coach us as well, but we just found out that you can't coach two teams, so—"

At this point Jimmy interrupted and said, "We want to advertise for a footy coach."

"… Exactly," said Chase.

"And how much did you want to spend?" asked Mr Watson.

Chase pulled out the money jar and tipped it upside down on the counter. "$7.50," he said.

Mr Watson stared at the collection of coins and said, "What did you want to say in the ad?"

Chase handed Mr Watson a piece of paper containing the ad that he and Jimmy had worked on.

Coach Wanted
Davinal Diggers U11 Football Team
Please send details to
idigthegig@wahoo.com
or
PO Box 117
Davinal

Mr Watson read it and smiled.

"Luckily for you we happen to be having a $7.50 special offer on ad placements this week," he said with a wink. "I'll make sure this is in tomorrow's paper."

The next morning Miles was in a great mood. He had found some chocolate that Mrs Winter had obviously been trying to hide from him, and he had nearly eaten the whole block.

He settled into his favourite arm chair, put his feet up on the coffee table and picked up the *Davinal Digest*. Splashed across the front page was the headline, "More Farmers Leave Davinal". Miles smiled as he scanned the accompanying article:

Bad luck and extreme drought conditions have forced two more farming families off their land this week, following problems with contaminated dam water. In both cases the land, which is

> currently worthless, was purchased by Selim
> Properties for a fraction of its original value ...

"Losers," he muttered to himself, flicking over to the financial pages. When he saw that the price of gold had risen overnight he started whistling. He stopped suddenly when he spotted Chase and Jimmy's ad.

Miles pulled out his mobile phone from the pocket of his silk dressing gown and quickly dialled a number.

"I think I see an opportunity you might like to apply for," he said. "Yes, it's on page 39 in the ad section of the *Davinal Digest*."

Miles hung up and smiled. It was only 9am but it had already been a very good day.

"Miles!" called out Mrs Winter from the kitchen.

Mr Winter rolled his eyes, "What?!"

"Have you seen the Laxettes I bought for Mace? He's been a bit blocked up lately. I left them in the medical cabinet next to your tablets."

Miles quickly looked at the wrapping paper of the chocolate he had been eating. Sure enough, the words "chocolate-flavoured laxative" appeared many times, but he had been too busy greedily gobbling it up to notice.

"No, I haven't seen them," he called out as his stomach started to churn.

"Don't panic," he said to himself, "you just need to make it to the toilet."

Miles got up and began slowly shuffling towards the nearest bathroom. He moved carefully, as he feared one false move could "open the floodgates", so to speak. He was very relieved to arrive at the bathroom door without making a mess. But when he tried the handle the door was locked.

"Someone's already in here!" yelled out Murdoch.

"It's a good thing we've got three toilets," thought Miles.

He was starting to sweat now, as his stomach was churning angrily and he knew he couldn't hold on for much longer.

A CHOCOLATE SURPRISE

"You're going to make it, you're going to make it," he kept telling himself.

He arrived at the second bathroom and frantically tried to open the door. The handle did not budge.

"I'm in here!" called out Magnus.

"You have got to be kidding me!" thought Miles.

His stomach was now producing loud gurgling noises, and to make matters worse the only remaining bathroom in the house was upstairs.

"You're going to make it! You're going to make it!" he told himself, taking it one step at a time.

He could see the bathroom down the hallway now and, to his great relief, the door was open. He slowly inched forward.

Three metres to go.

"You're going to make it!"

Two metres to go.

"You're going to make it!"

One metre to go.

"So close now—you're going to make it!"

All of a sudden, Mace flew out of his bedroom, pushed passed his father and shot into the bathroom, slamming the door behind him.

"You snooze, you lose!" he called out to his father from behind the locked door.

Miles stared at the door and thought, "You're *not* going to make it."

The explosive sound that followed was so loud it woke up the neighbour's baby.

11

Weeding Out the Problems

"This is a catastrophe!" said Chase. "A C-A-T ... umm ... It's a catastrophe!"

Fox always tried to be positive, but this time he agreed with his brother. Only one person had applied to coach the Davinal under-11s—and that person was Mr Percy!

"Maybe he won't be so bad?" said Fox unconvincingly.

"And maybe Dad will win a **Brownlow Medal!**" said Chase.

"Hey, maybe I could!" said Mr Swift, who had been walking past Chase's bedroom. "By the way, what's a Brownlow thingy?"

Fox and Chase looked at each other and laughed.

"Trust Dad to make Mr Percy look good!" said Fox.

Chase's worst fears about Mr Percy were confirmed the next day at school. On his way back to class after recess, he and Jimmy overheard their new coach talking on his mobile phone to a friend.

"... Oh, I hate footy. In fact the only thing I hate more is children. I only took the stupid coaching job so I can say I'm helping the community ... Yeah, so I can get a real job in the city. Davinal is full of hillbillies and the kids are all spoilt brats ... Yeah really dumb, and *so boring* ... Oh hey, have I told you about the giant kiwi fruit I'm growing?"

Chase had heard enough. He was already extremely suspicious that Mr Percy had arranged for the under-11 players to meet on his front lawn for their first training session.

"Maybe he's going to make us do a **time trial?**" said Jimmy.

"And maybe I'll get 100 per cent in the next spelling test," said Chase.

Jimmy burst out laughing, "100 per cent in a spelling test—good one, Chase!"

"No need to laugh quite so hard," said Chase.

WEEDING OUT THE PROBLEMS

All the under-11s Diggers players turned up for training in Mr Percy's front yard at 4pm sharp. The only one who was late was Mr Percy.

"How can he be late?" cried Chase. "He lives here!"

Finally, at about quarter past four, Mr Percy emerged from his house, drinking through a long, twisting whacky straw from a large, purple plastic cup. He was wearing red tracksuit pants and a ridiculously tight fluorescent-orange T-shirt that said "Vegetables have rights too". To top off his ensemble, he was wearing a yellow headband. Even though he hadn't been doing any exercise, there was a thin line of sweat under his equally thin moustache.

"Okay, everyone, find your own space on the grass. We're going to start with a warm-up," he said taking a noisy slurp of his drink.

The group of about 20 kids did as they were instructed. Chase, who assumed their coach was about to give them some stretching exercises, thought maybe he had been wrong about Mr Percy.

"Now, crouch down onto your knees," said Mr Percy, "and start weeding."

"Weeding?" said Chase

"Yes, pull out any weeds you see while you're kneeling."

"But how is that going to—"

"Uh, uh, uh! All will be revealed later," said Mr Percy mysteriously.

The rest of the training involved the kids washing windows, raking up leaves and watering plants. At one stage, as the young team was filling up the foul-smelling compost bin, Chase looked over at Mr Percy. He was sitting in a deckchair eating a muffin.

Every time the players asked their coach why they were doing gardening jobs, Mr Percy would respond, "It will be all become clear."

Mr Percy had stolen this idea from a movie he had once seen called *The Karate Kid*. In this film an old Japanese guy trained a young boy in martial arts by getting him to paint his fence, wash his car and sand his patio. As it turned out, by doing all these repetitive chores, the boy was really learning how to become a karate champion. The major difference here was that the chores Mr Percy was giving to his players did not help their footballing skills at all. He just wanted to get someone to do his gardening for free.

Meanwhile, the Diggers under-14s team was also having its first training session of the season—except this one was taking place on an actual football oval.

Fox was so happy to be back at the Diggers' home ground he couldn't stop smiling. As soon as he walked into the changing rooms he was greeted by Mr Scott, who seemed just as excited as his players about the start of a new season. Fox thought his coach looked even fitter than last year, and remembered how Mrs Swift had said that Mr Scott and his girlfriend, Samantha Lu, were getting on very well. She had also told him that Mr Scott had started writing articles for a national newspaper.

"I didn't know you were a writer, Mr Scott," said Fox.

"Anyone can be a writer, Fox," said Mr Scott. "All you need is a pen, some paper and a few ideas."

"What do you write about?"

"Mainly stories about playing footy in the bush. People seem to really like them, and now someone wants to put them in a book."

"That is so cool," said Fox.

When all the players had changed and were on the oval, Mr Scott called them into a huddle and welcomed them back to the club. He also thanked Lewis for agreeing to be the team's runner again.

"I'm just doing it for the children," said Lewis, doing a perfect impersonation of Mr Winter that caused everyone to laugh.

Mr Scott then introduced them all to Aslam, who was the Diggers' only new player, and everyone clapped loudly. Some kids yelled out, "On ya, Laser!" while others called out, "Great stuff, Khany!" and Fox thought about how rare it was in Australia to call anyone by their real name.

Mr Scott also introduced Laser to Joey and Gary, who had hopped over to the huddle not wanting to be left out.

"I want to start off the year with a brand-new footy drill that Cyril Rioli has sent through," said Mr Scott.

Aslam turned to Fox in disbelief and said, "*Cyril Rioli* sends you guys training drills—seriously?!"

Fox grinned and nodded.

"This is the greatest football club ever!" said Aslam as he gently patted Joey behind her ear.

Mr Scott explained Cyril's new drill, which was called "Hunting in Packs".

"Okay, I need you to divide up into four groups. One group line up behind the giant pumpkin, one behind the large leek, one behind the pumped-up potato, and one behind the big beetroot."

WEEDING OUT THE PROBLEMS

The players sprinted over to the four oversized vegetables—leftover from when Mr Percy was coach and now used as witches' hats—and quickly formed queues of approximately equal length behind each.

"The player at the front in the potato group has to **paddle the ball** in front of them to where I am standing," continued Mr Scott. "When they get halfway to me, the player at the front of the beetroot line has to try to tackle that player, and the player at the front of the leek line has to try to protect the 'paddler' by shepherding. When the paddler gets to me, they are allowed to pick up the ball, and the person at the front of the pumpkin line has to time their run so that they receive a handball from the paddler as soon as they pick the ball up. Is that clear?"

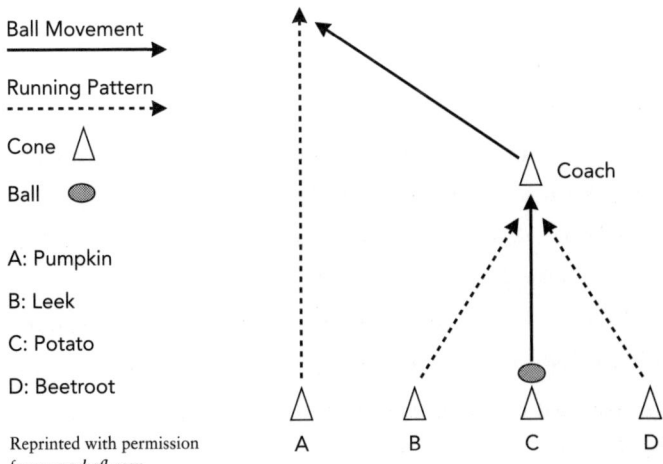

Reprinted with permission from *coachafl.com*

Fox thought an outsider listening in on what Mr Scott was saying would be totally confused, but for some reason his explanations of drills involving enormous vegetables made perfect sense to his young team.

The Diggers all threw themselves into training. Fox was rapt to see Mo put the troubles on his farm behind him and deliver his torpedo punt passes as accurately as ever. He watched Paige, Chung, Rosie, Simon, Bruno, Sammy, Chris, and Aslam all train brilliantly. He also noticed how much the other players in the team had improved over the past two years. It was obvious the Diggers were going to have a sensational side again. He glanced over at Hugo, who was clearly loving the freedom of not having to wear his bodysuit—he actually seemed to enjoy it when he fell on the ground. At the end of training, he even lay down on his back, waved his arms back and forth and yelled out, "Grass Angels!"

Lewis came over to him and, sounding very concerned, said, "Hugo, your face is really—"

"Swollen?!" said Hugo in a panic.

"No, ugly!" said Lewis with a big grin.

Hugo burst out laughing and gave his mate a high five.

"You got me, Lewis," he said.

WEEDING OUT THE PROBLEMS

At school the next day Fox was having lunch with Lewis, Hugo and Chase near the school's administration building. He had just noticed that there was now a giant hole in the wall next to the principal's office, when Miss Carey suddenly appeared in the middle of it wearing safety goggles and holding a sledgehammer. She knocked out a few more bricks with the sledgehammer then ducked back inside through the hole.

It was possibly the only time Fox had seen Lewis speechless. He looked at his best mate and said, "Termites."

As they ate their sandwiches, Chase complained about Mr Percy's training session.

"—and to make it even worse, at the end of the night he called me 'Dingo' in front of everyone."

"Dingo?" said Lewis.

"He said that because my brother was Fox, I might as well be called Dingo."

"At least he remembers who you are," said Hugo. Mr Percy had constantly forgotten Hugo's name when he'd been coach of the Diggers, even though Hugo was the only player who wore a bodysuit.

"And next week he said we have to polish his giant potatoes," moaned Chase. Fox had never seen his brother look so miserable.

All of a sudden, Hugo shut his eyes, put his fingertips to his temples and slowly started rubbing them in small circles. Then his eyes popped opened.

"I think I've got an idea," he said.

12

Coaching Secrets

Hugo's plan was simple.

"Chase, if the under-11s are okay with it, I could take them for a secret training session once a week."

Chase thought this was a brilliant idea. All the kids had been impressed with Hugo when he'd taken them for drills in the backyard, so he knew they would agree.

"And as the under-11s will be playing before the under-14s at the same ground, I could give you guys some suggestions during your games—"

"So you'd be like our secret coach!" said Chase enthusiastically.

"Well I don't know whether 'coach' is the right—"

"Thanks heaps, Coach," said Chase. "And don't worry, Mr Percy is so clueless about football he won't know what's going on."

Hugo's coaching plan was given a boost by Lewis, who approached Mr Percy and offered to be the runner for the under-11s. Mr Percy, who had no idea what a runner did, agreed immediately so he wouldn't look foolish.

The under-11s really enjoyed the training sessions with Hugo, and having him as their secret coach made game day even more exciting.

Just before the start of the first game, Mr Percy announced that Dingo would be the team's captain.

"My name is *Chase*!"

"Whatevs," said Mr Percy. The reason he had made Chase captain was because Dingo was the only name in the group he could remember.

"How could he *not* know our names?" asked Jimmy after Mr Percy had called him "Hey you!" for the ninth time. "He taught most of us at school last year!"

When the season got underway, the under-11s quickly came up with a system. Hugo would stand in the huddle during the breaks and say things to the players out of the corner of his mouth like, "Soobs, if you can't take a mark in the backline, make sure you spoil the ball." He would also go around the huddle patting players on the back and reminding them about the good things they had done during the previous quarter. Hugo even made positional changes during a game by discreetly telling Lewis which players to bring on and off the ground.

Mr Percy was completely unaware of Hugo's secret role, because during the games he was always preoccupied with reading magazines with names like *Colossal Carrots Monthly* and *Songs to Sing to Your Celery*. And at the end of each quarter, instead of talking about football, Mr Percy would spend the whole time complaining about things, like the poor quality of caffè lattes in Davinal.

Fox really enjoyed watching Chase, Jimmy and their friends playing before his under-14s games. They were such an exciting team he almost didn't want to go into the rooms to get changed at three-quarter time. Chase and Jimmy were electrifying onballers. They would win the footy all over the ground and as soon as they gathered possession they would instinctively look for each other. One of Fox's favourite passages of play was when Chase and Jimmy handballed to each other all the way up the field from the back pocket, before Jimmy snapped an easy goal from **point-blank range**.

The under-11s ruckman, Gregor 'The Burpinator' Ivanisovich, was unstoppable. Opposition rucks were too frightened to go up against him and he would either palm the ball to Chase and Jimmy, or simply smash it with his fist into the forward line. In one of the early games when Davinal had the breeze, Gregor thumped the football so hard it carried all the way through to score a behind!

The super cool Zebidiah Fontaine, turned out to be a freakish full-forward, **kicking a bag** of 11 goals in the first game against the Colbran Cockatoos. What amazed Fox was that even though Zeb would kick goal after goal, he never looked like he was really trying.

As Fox suspected, Masumi Kato played a lot like Paige Turner. She too was a deadly accurate kick for goal on either foot. Not only was she able to kick goals from any angle, but she also made life easy for her teammates by giving them worm-burner passes.

Minoo 'Mini' Saaed thrilled the crowd every week by taking some absolute screamers. On one occasion she literally jumped over an opponent to take a mark. Fox was convinced she was going to be an Australian high jump champion in the future.

Subin Wek, or 'Soobs' as everyone called her, was one of those gifted athletes who could run fast, and run fast *all day*. She would take a saving mark in defence, and less than a minute later would receive a handball in the forward pocket and kick a goal. Fox predicted that Soobs was also destined for the Olympics.

Adesh Gupta was the under-11s full-back, and with his long arms he was able to spoil any of the full-forwards he came up against. He also seemed indestructible, as any time he was crunched in a tackle he would always bounce straight back up.

But without a doubt, Fox's favourite under-11s player was Johnny Ticker. 'JT' may have been missing a large part of his left arm, but he had incredible balance and a spectacular leap. Not only did he regularly take one-handed hangers, he also never stopped running and went in for the ball harder than anyone Fox had ever seen. During one of their regular dinnertime footy conversations, the Swift brothers had agreed that JT was the gutsiest player on the planet. Mrs Swift had suggested that "bravest" or "most courageous" were better terms to use.

"Or how about 'valiant' or 'plucky'?" said Mr Swift.

"I think we'll stick with gutsiest," said Chase.

Just like the under-11s, the Diggers under-14s started the season brilliantly. They were winning games by more than 10 goals each week and what Fox enjoyed more than anything was linking arms with his teammates after the game and singing the Diggers club song.

Oh we're from Diggerland
A fighting fury, we're from Diggerland
In any weather you will see us with a grin
Risking head and skin
If we're behind, then never mind we'll fight and fight and win
For we're from Diggerland
We never weaken 'til the final siren's gone
Like the Diggers of old
We're strong and we're bold
Oh we're from Digger ...
YELLOW AND BLUE
For we're from Diggerland!

It had quickly become a tradition for Lewis to squirt water over everyone when they yelled out, "YELLOW AND BLUE!"

Every week a large group of loyal supporters would come and watch the Diggers play. Fox's favourite supporters were the two oldies, Snowy Davidson and Matilda Wall, who never missed a game. Matilda had even made a tiny cape in Diggers colours for her rabbit Gary to wear while leading out the team with Joey. When he dashed onto the field, the cape would stretch out behind him, making him look like a superhero.

SUPERHARE-O

Even though the Diggers were winning easily, Fox found that the opposition players were usually very friendly after the game. There were some familiar faces from last year, such as Rob 'The Birdman' Stewart, 'Jacko' Jackson, 'Lightning' Lucas, 'Roady' Rodan, Seb 'Westy' Westin and the always smiling Ed Gillies. Jacko, Lightning and Roady were all still deeply embarrassed about playing for the Dragons last year.

"Fox, can you just pretend last year never happened?" said Roady with a smile after the Diggers' game against the Romana Roosters.

There were also some new stars in the competition who were really nice to chat to, like Patrick 'Strawbs' O'Dwyer from the Stonewarren Stingrays and Alice 'Naso' Nason and Georgia 'Panos' Paine from the Ballymore Bears.

Another change this season was that Mr Scott had started bringing jelly snakes for the players to eat at three-quarter time for an energy boost. Lewis would bring out bowls of different-coloured snakes, and everyone would rush over and try to grab a couple of their favourite flavours.

"Itzlykhungshephitinovabalohe," said Mo shaking his head.

"It is a bit like hungry sheep fighting over a bale of hay," said Paige, translating Mo's mumbled words for Fox's benefit.

The main on-field improvement for the Diggers came about thanks to Aslam playing on the half-back flank, where he combined brilliantly with Mo and Bruno. As soon as one of these key position players would take a mark, Laser would flash by, receive the handball, take a bounce, and then deliver the ball onto the chest of a Diggers player deep in the forward line.

Aslam moved the ball down the field so quickly Mr Scott said it was like watching a slingshot being fired.

COACHING SECRETS

The Diggers were undefeated when it came to round five, when they came up against the Davinal Drongos.

The game was at the Drongos' home ground, but Fox no longer felt like this was a disadvantage for the Diggers. He trusted his teammates to perform well wherever they played and in any conditions.

As usual, Fox arrived very early so he could watch Chase and his friends play. While the under-11s changed into their footy gear, Fox picked up a *Record* off the bench and checked out the under-14s ladder.

	P	W	L	Pts	%
Davinal Diggers	4	4	0	16	236
Shepton Sharks	4	3	1	12	205
Colbran Cockatoos	4	3	1	12	148
Romana Roosters	4	3	1	12	142
Davinal Drongos	4	3	1	12	120
Stonewarren Stingrays	4	2	2	8	124
Ballymore Bears	4	2	2	8	116
Tennant Hill Tigers	4	2	2	4	113
Gregtown Goannas	4	2	2	8	76
Firbush Fever	4	0	4	4	50
Morgan Bridge Magpies	4	0	4	0	36
Linmore Leopards	4	0	4	0	22

With all the paid players going back to their original clubs, the Drongos were nowhere near as good as they were last year. They had already lost a game to the Stonewarren Stingrays, and some of their wins had only been by narrow margins.

All the same, Fox was still expecting a close, hard-fought game—so he was very surprised when the Diggers were able to get on top right from the start. He was also amazed that Mr Winter kept his cool for the entire four quarters. Even when the lol-ing kookaburra that had driven him over the edge last year started laughing every time the Diggers kicked a goal, Miles merely shrugged his shoulders, checked his smartphone and said, "At least the price of gold is going up."

Mace played very well against the Diggers, but he was always trying to do too much on his own and as a result was **caught holding the ball** three times—once by Rosie, once by Chung and, best of all, once by Hugo!

"You're too good for him, 'Dangerman'!" yelled out Lewis.

Hugo loved it when his teammates called him Dangerman, but Lewis' comment sent Mace into a fit of rage. He threw the ball at Hugo's head, which resulted in a costly 25-metre penalty against him, setting up Hugo in the goalsquare. With Mace still complaining to the umpire about the decision, Hugo lined up to take his shot. He **kicked truly**, slotting his second goal in three years, and his teammates rushed in from all over the field to congratulate him.

When the siren sounded to end the game, the scoreboard read:

| Drongos | 4.7 (31) |
| Visitors | 18.13 (121) |

As the Diggers walked into the changing rooms and hurried over to grab any leftover snakes, Fox noticed that Lewis was putting a sign up on the wall.

It read, "Hugo is **Falcon** Free for ... Matches".

Lewis then stuck the number "5" in the blank space and gave the smiling Hugo a pat on the back.

"I will be updating this sign every week," he announced. "And by the way, how good was Hugo's tackle on Mace?"

Everyone cheered and Hugo went bright red.

Fox sat on the bench in the changing rooms and looked around at his laughing teammates. He thought, "Winning easily every week is good, but ..."

Mr Scott must have been reading his mind, because he sat down next to Fox and said, "I think we need to change things up a little."

Fox smiled. He had no idea what his coach had planned, but he couldn't wait to find out.

13

Fast Changes

A week later, Mr Scott stood quietly beside the whiteboard in the changing rooms. The players were all sitting on the benches waiting for their coach to talk to them before they ran out to take on the Linmore Leopards.

Fox noticed that the whiteboard had been covered up so that nobody could see what was written on it.

FAST CHANGES

When Mr Scott finally did his dramatic unveiling, the Diggers players all gasped in shock.

On the whiteboard was a diagram of a football oval with the players' names and their positions for the game.

"I think you made a few typos, Mr Scott!" called out Lewis.

According to the whiteboard, Fox was to line up at full-back, Mo at full-forward, Bruno in the ruck, Simon at centre half-back, Paige in the back pocket, Chung on a back flank, Rosie in the forward pocket, and Chris and Sammy on the wings.

"Today there are going to be a few changes," announced Mr Scott.

Fox smiled. He knew that their coach was trying to keep things interesting for the players. Hugo smiled, too, because he was going to start as the **ruck-rover**!

"I know I am asking all of you to play in positions you have never played in before," said Mr Scott. "But don't worry—I expect you to make mistakes. All I want you to do is learn as much as you can about playing whatever role I give you each week."

Fox had an idea and put up his hand.

"Yes, Fox?" said Mr Scott.

"How about we also have a different captain every game? That way a different person gets to toss the coin and lead out the team each week."

Mr Scott smiled. "I think that's a great idea, Fox—but it's something the whole team has to agree on."

Hugo put up his hand.

"Yes, Hugo?" said Mr Scott.

"I reckon that would be really cool, as long as Fox is locked in as our captain if we make the finals."

The players all nodded in agreement.

"Okay, that means we need someone to be our captain for today," said Mr Scott. "Who's it going to be?"

"I nominate Hugo," said Lewis.

"I second that," said Chung.

"Is everyone happy with that choice?" asked the coach.

All the players nodded their heads and murmured their approval.

"Hugo, you are officially the captain of the Diggers for today!" said Mr Scott.

Hugo nearly fainted. He had often dreamed about being the captain of a team, but had never thought it would actually happen. He wanted to say something inspirational, but was so overwhelmed he became completely tongue-tied.

"I um, er, well, that's, um, wow, er—"

"What Hugo means to say," said Paige, "is that he's really honoured to be the captain, and we all have to go in really hard against Linmore today!"

"Yeah, that!" said Hugo.

FAST CHANGES

Everyone laughed and Hugo high-fived Paige to thank her for coming to the rescue.

Hugo led the team out, giving a small wave to his mum, dad and sister in the crowd. His family was surprised but very proud as they watched him go over and shake hands with the Leopards captain and then be part of the coin toss.

Once the game started, the Diggers made a lot of mistakes, just as Mr Scott had predicted, and as a result Lewis was kept busy running out the coach's messages to the players.

"Simon, Mr Scott says that in the backline you can't always fly for marks. If your opponent is in a better position you need to spoil."

Fox did a great job on the Linmore full-forward, even though his opponent was at least 10cm taller than him. He managed to keep his player goalless and to **run off him** to set up play downfield.

Lewis kept Fox entertained throughout the game by pretending he thought he was the Diggers' usual full-back, Mo Officer.

"Mo, you've shrunk! Look at those puny arms—how are you supposed to pick up a tractor with those chicken wings?!"

"Lewis, stop making me laugh, I'm trying to concentrate!" said Fox.

Lewis looked up to sky and put on an American accent, "Mo, I can finally understand what you're saying, man! It's a miracle! A miracle!"

The Diggers won the game against the Leopards by only 39 points, their smallest margin of the season, but Mr Scott wasn't upset at all. In fact over the next few weeks he continued to set the players different challenges to keep everyone on their toes. Fox was asked to tag the opposition's best onballer, Paige and Chung both played in key positions, Rosie went to full-forward, and Mo became possibly the biggest rover to ever play junior football.

Mr Scott wanted some other ideas to keep his players fresh and alert, so he emailed Cyril Rioli and explained what he had been up to.

FAST CHANGES

Later that night, the Diggers coach checked his inbox and smiled when he saw Cyril's reply.

Hey Greg,

What you're doing with the Diggers sounds really cool. Mixing it up like that is pretty much what we do at Hawthorn. It's great you have players learning to play in different positions because, as our coach Alastair Clarkson says, 'If one soldier goes down, there's always another one to take their place'. If some teams lose a full-back they have no one else who knows how to play in that position—imagine if that happened the week before the Grand Final!

One training routine (and we also do it pre-game as well) is a group of four players, all close together, doing rapid handballs. This encourages team play and also sharpens up the hands for one-grab gathers and disposals. It's a fast, fun way to start training, and before the game it sharpens the reflexes and calms the nerves!

Hope this helps!

All the best,

Cyril.

PS Go Diggers! (And Hawks!)

Mr Scott loved the idea of the fast handballs drill—and so did the players.

"Cyril, you've done it again," thought Fox with a smile as he, Chung, Rosie and Chris fired rapid handballs at each other just before the game against the Gregtown Goannas.

In this game, Mr Scott asked Aslam to play on the ball. Fox knew this would not be a problem for Laser, because he was such a fast, fit and creative player. But by early on in the second half, Fox could tell that Laser was struggling to keep up with his opponent. Mr Scott noticed it as well, and at the three-quarter time break he took Aslam aside and asked him if he needed a rest. Aslam said he was fine, but halfway through the last quarter he looked pale and seemed to have no energy at all. Fox was concerned for his teammate, and after the game went up to him to see what was wrong.

"Hey Laser, are you okay?"

Aslam took a deep breath and said, "I'm feeling a bit dizzy."

"What's the matter, do you have a cold?" asked Fox.

"No, it's Ramadan."

"Ramadan? That sounds serious!" said Fox. "Is it contagious?"

Despite feeling terrible, Aslam burst out laughing.

Fox turned to Hugo, who was sitting next to him, and said, "What's so funny? What's Ramadan?"

"It's the ninth month of the Muslim year," said Hugo. "It's a holy month when Muslims fast from dawn to sunset."

"Fast?"

"As in don't eat."

"Ohhh!" said Fox, turning back to Aslam. "So you haven't had any breakfast? No wonder you didn't have any energy out there today!"

Fox remembered all the Diggers players munching on lolly snakes at three-quarter time. He thought that watching everyone else eat when you're really hungry couldn't be much fun.

All of a sudden a name popped into Fox's head. "Leave it with me, Laser. I may have an idea."

"Bachar Houli!" said Fox.

"Bachar Houli?" repeated Chase.

"The star Richmond player."

"Derr! I know who Bachar Houli is," said Chase. Like Fox, he knew every player at every AFL club.

"He's a Muslim."

"So?"

"So I want to find out how he manages to play footy during Ramadan! That way maybe Laser can do the same."

"Oh, that's brilliant!"

"Thanks Chase," said Fox, rolling his eyes.

Fox typed the words "Bachar Houli" and "Ramadan" into his computer's search engine and up popped a link to a blog article the Tigers star had written about his diet during Ramadan.

> My diet doesn't change much during Ramadan, just the times of day and portions that I eat. Here is an insight into a typical week of eating during Ramadan …

Fox read on and started smiling. "This is perfect," he said. "Muslims need to fast between dawn and dusk, but Azza could do what Bachar Houli does."

"Which is what?" asked Chase.

"Set his alarm early and eat before the sun comes up," explained Fox.

"And he should drink some extra fluids and maybe a sports drink before dawn, too," said Chase, reading over his brother's shoulder.

The next week against the Shepton Sharks, Mr Scott gave Aslam another opportunity to play in the midfield. It turned out to be the best game of football that Laser had played in his life. He ran all day, picking up kicks all over the ground and even managing to slot three goals.

After the game Lewis put up the number "7" in the space on Hugo's number of falcon-free matches poster, and squirted everyone with water as they yelled out

FAST CHANGES

"YELLOW AND BLUE!" during the club song.

Aslam, who had never sung the song so loudly and had a giant grin on his face, suddenly realised that there had been something different about this game.

"Where were the lolly snakes at three-quarter time?" he said.

"We all agreed, no snakes for anyone until after Ramadan," said Fox.

"How come?" said Aslam.

Fox shrugged his shoulders. "Because you're a mate," he said.

14

Oink, Oink

Mr Scott was typing up a story about his old playing days with the Diggers when he heard the familiar *ping* of a new email arriving in his inbox.

"Maybe Cyril is sending through another drill," he thought.

He quickly flicked to his email page, and stared at the name of the sender.

"Barry Magro?! What the heck does *he* want?"

Barry Magro had played against Mr Scott many years ago when they were both teenagers. Barry had been captain of the Tennant Hill Tigers and was always very jealous of Greg Scott's natural ability. Unlike Mr Scott, Barry Magro was never invited to train with any of the clubs in the Big League, and this had really upset him. Barry ended up becoming a PE teacher and now spent a lot of time at the gym—mostly admiring himself in the big mirrors. In fact his nickname ever since his teenage years had been 'Gigjam', which stood for "Gee I'm Good, Just Ask Me!"

About 10 years ago, Barry had started coaching junior football teams. His teams were very successful and, as a result, he had recently been given the job of coaching the combined under-14s metropolitan team. This team was made up of all the best junior footballers in the city, of which a number were predicted to go on to become champions of the game.

Mr Scott scrolled down and read Barry's email.

FOX SWIFT AND THE GOLDEN BOOT

Dear Greg,

Long time no speak. As you would have heard, my coaching career has really taken off and I am now in charge of the state metropolitan under-14s team. (A lot of people applied for this job, including several ex-AFL players, but they chose me.) I heard the other day that you were coaching the Davinal Diggers under-14s and that they were doing okay. My team needs some practice before the State Championships, so I was hoping you could put together a combined team from your local league to take us on. It probably won't give my players much competition, but an easy win would give my team a confidence boost before going into the Championships. I contacted the president of your league (Mabel Hurley) and she said we could play your competition's "all-star" team during the week of your league's upcoming bye, and that you would be the coach. Of course, if you are too scared to accept this challenge I will understand completely. Not all of us are cut out to be amazing coaches. I guess I was just lucky.

All the best,

Barry Magro
State Metro Under-14s Coach

Mr Scott shook his head. He was amazed how many times Barry could say "I" and "my" in one short email. He shot off a three-word response and pressed send:

Game on, GIGJAM.

Barry Magro hated being called Gigjam, and his left eye started twitching when he read Mr Scott's reply.

"No one calls me Gigjam any more! I am going to crush you like a bug, Scott," he said out loud.

At that precise moment, a small bug appeared on the desk next to his computer. Barry raised his fist and brought it crashing down on the table. Unfortunately for him, the insect flew off at the last second and the only thing he crushed was his hand, which started to swell immediately. When he arrived at the hospital, the doctor shook her head and told him he had broken a bone and would be in a sling for three weeks.

Barry's eye started twitching again. "You'll pay for this, Scott," he said. "You will so pay for this."

A week later the story on the front page of the *Davinal Digest* was "Local Juniors to take on City Superstars". Fox and Chase were in the kitchen together studying the article, which included a list of the under-14s players who would be representing the district as well as the name of their home club:

Ballymore Bears (2): Alice Nason, Georgia Paine
Colbran Cockatoos (1): Daryl Jackson
Davinal Diggers (10): Bruno Gallucci, Aslam Khan, Chung Lee, Rosie McHusky, Simon Phillips, Robert Officer, Samir Saaed, Francis Swift, Paige Turner, Chriz Wek
Davinal Drongos (4): Angelo Blunt, Vince Brogan, Sandy Barr, Mace Winter
Linmore Leopards (1): Brendan White
Romana Roosters (2): Edward Gillies, Peter Rodan
Stonewarren Stingrays (3): Patrick O'Dwyer, Robert Stewart, Sebastian Westin
Tennant Hill Tigers (1): Anthony Lucas

"How awesome will it be to play with Rob 'The Birdman' Stewart instead of against him?" said Fox.

"Yeah, but you also have to play with Mace and Vince," said Chase.

"Thanks for reminding me, bro!"

Fox read the rest of the article, which went on to explain that the district had never been represented by a combined side before. As a result, the *Davinal Digest* was running a competition where people could send in their suggestions for the new team's name and a jumper design.

"Cool!" said Chase. "Unless they come up with a name like the Drongos."

OINK, OINK

Fox was very excited about the first training session for the combined side, which was held at the Diggers' home ground. Apart from Mace, everyone was extremely friendly.

Alice 'Naso' Nason and Georgia 'Panos' Paine were two of the main reasons that the Ballymore Bears had improved so much this year. These two **goal sneaks** both had long blonde hair and looked very similar—so much so that Fox initially thought they were sisters. As it turned out, Alice and Paige were good mates from gymnastics, and Georgia, who was a very fast sprinter, knew Rosie through athletics.

Fox also really enjoyed chatting to the giant red head Patrick 'Strawbs' O'Dwyer from the Stonewarren Stingrays. Strawbs was fearless on the footy field and would always yell out encouragement to his teammates. Many of his opponents were quite scared of him because he had **white line fever**, but off the field Fox discovered he was a softly spoken boy who sang in the Stonewarren church choir every Sunday. Like Fox, Strawbs was very excited about being selected for the combined team.

Mr Scott called for everyone's attention and put a large box on the table next to him.

"Welcome everyone, I am really looking forward to getting to know you all. First things first, this team needs a name, so it is my great pleasure to introduce to you the winner of the *Davinal Digest* Name the Team competition—Mr Lewis Rioli."

Fox's eyes nearly popped out of his head when Lewis strolled into changing rooms and went and stood next to Mr Scott.

Everyone started clapping and whistling except for Mace, who folded his arms and put on a grumpy face.

"Thank you, thank you very much. You are too kind—except for *you*," he said, pointing at Mace, which made everyone laugh.

"Because this area was settled mainly thanks to gold mining, I thought the best name for the team was—"

Lewis opened up the box he was holding and reached inside.

"The Nuggets!" he said, pulling out the jumper he had designed and holding it up for everyone to see. The players all jumped up and high-fived each other.

OINK, OINK

"That is so cool, Lewis!" said Fox.

The jumper was red with a gold collar and the team's emblem, a gold nugget, was in the middle. Lewis also held up a pair of socks that had red and gold hoops.

"Thanks, Lewis," said Mr Scott. "So our team now has a jumper—the next thing we need is a captain."

Most of the players turned to stare at Fox.

"Do we have any nominations?"

Ed Gillies, who was the captain of the Romana Roosters, raised his hand and said, "I nominate Fox Swift."

There was a lot of head nodding and murmurs of approval from the other players.

Vince thought back to the nominations for school captain, and how upset Mace had been with him.

"Do you want me to nominate you?" he whispered to Mace.

"No way, you idiot—I don't want to go through that embarrassment again!" Mace could not believe how stupid Vince was, and decided to teach him a lesson. So he raised his hand and said, "I nominate Vince."

"Ha!" thought Mace. "Vince will look so stupid when he doesn't get a vote."

"Any more nominations?" asked Mr Scott. "No? Okay, who votes for Fox?"

Every player in the changing rooms put up their hand—including Mace and Vince!

"What a complete loser!" thought Mace, looking at Vince.

"Well that makes Fox our captain," said Mr Scott, causing everyone to clap and cheer.

"And Vince, that makes you the vice-captain."

"What?!" said Mace.

A huge smile broke out on Vince's face. "Hey thanks for the nomination, Mace," he said, patting his friend on the back.

"Shut up, Vince!"

After handing out all the jumpers and socks to the players, Mr Scott revealed the starting positions for the upcoming game against the metropolitan team.

"Wait a minute!" yelled out Mace.

"What's the matter?" asked Mr Scott.

"You've got me on a half-back flank and McHusky on the ball! I'm a much better player than her—you only put her there because she's a Digger."

"The last thing I want is any of you thinking I'm playing favourites," said Mr Scott. "How about if you and Rosie do some one-on-one contests tonight at training, and whoever performs better will start off as ruck-rover?"

"Fine with me," said Rosie.

"And *absolutely* fine with me," said Mace. He then went over to the corner and started changing into his footy gear away from the other players. Vince followed him and watched as he took a small jar of Vaseline out of his bag and began rubbing it all over his shoulders and arms.

"What are you doing?" asked Vince.

"When McHusky tries to tackle me, she'll slip right off," said Mace.

Chung wandered over and started to get changed next to Mace and Vince.

"Best of luck out there, Mace," he said. "I'm sure you'll do well."

"What are you, Chung—a fortune cookie? Get lost!" said Mace.

Mace looked across at Vince expecting him to be laughing at his joke. He was very annoyed to see Vince staring at him blankly.

"It's funny because he's Asian and I called him a fortune cookie," explained Mace.

But Vince continued to look confused.

"My jokes are way too clever for you, Vince," said Mace, shaking his head.

"Oh, *now* I get it," said Vince, bursting out laughing.

Mace smiled.

"Chung is really smart and wise, like a fortune cookie," said Vince.

"Shut up, Vince!"

Before heading out to the oval, Mace put an extra glob of Vaseline on his hands and applied another layer to his arms just to be safe.

Early on in the training session, while the rest of the players did some circle work, Mr Scott took Mace and Rosie to one side.

"Let's start off by seeing what you're both like at taking an overhead mark," he said.

Mace chuckled to himself. In his mind, he *had* to be better at overhead marking than Rosie.

Mr Scott kicked the first ball to Rosie, who kept her eyes on the footy and marked it cleanly and confidently overhead.

Mace was secretly impressed, but whispered to Rosie, "Pfft! As if taking a mark on your own takes any skill."

Mr Scott then kicked the ball to Mace.

"Piece of cake," he thought as he lined himself up with the flight of the ball and put his arms in the air.

Unfortunately Mace's hands were still completely covered in Vaseline, and the ball slipped straight through them and hit him on the head.

"Hey, I thought Hugo was the Falcon King!" called out Lewis from the boundary, once again causing everyone to laugh.

"The sun got in my eye!" explained Mace.

"But the sun's behind you, Ma—"

"Shut up, Vince!"

"Okay, Rosie and Mace, we're going to try something else," said Mr Scott. "I'm going to kick the footy about 30 metres and I want you two to chase after it, compete for it, then deliver the ball back to me accurately with a kick or a handball. Is that clear?"

Rosie and Mace nodded. Mr Scott then kicked the ball over their heads and they immediately turned and dashed after it. Being an elite runner, Rosie arrived at the ball metres before Mace. She picked it up, neatly dodged around her greasy opponent, took a bounce and then speared a pass back onto Mr Scott's chest.

The other players all gave Rosie a clap and Lewis yelled out, "I hope you like dust, Mace, because you're eating a lot of Rosie's!"

The two players ran back to Mr Scott, who noticed Mace was breathing much more heavily than Rosie.

"Hey, no fair, Mr Scott," panted Mace. "You kicked that one to McHusky's advantage!"

Mr Scott then kicked the ball more to the side that Mace was standing on, giving him a clear advantage this time. But just as Mace was about to swoop on the ball he felt a breeze rush past him. That breeze was Rosie, who scooped up the ball and spun around to face him.

Mace was determined not to let her baulk him this time. Not only was he going to tackle her, he was going to drive her into the ground—and if he hurt her it would serve her right for making him look stupid.

But Rosie did something completely unexpected. Instead of baulking around Mace, she did a tiny chip kick just over his head. Mace leapt up to intercept it, but the ball sailed just over his fingertips.

In a flash, Rosie sprinted past him and marked the ball before it hit the ground, then she took a bounce and handballed it back Mr Scott. The Nuggets all nodded their heads and clapped in appreciation.

"You got da moves, girl!" said Lewis in his best American accent.

"One more time!" demanded Mace. "Just give me one more chance!"

"Fine by me," said Rosie with a smile.

Mace knew there was only one way he could get to the footy before Rosie, and that was by cheating. So the next time Mr Scott kicked the ball, he tripped Rosie just as she took off and laughed as she fell to the ground.

This time, with a 10-metre head start, Mace was first to the ball.

"All I have to do is dodge around McHusky and shoot a pass onto Mr Scott's chest—this'll be too easy," thought Mace.

He moved one way and then the other, but he couldn't fool Rosie—she grabbed his arms and the ball spilled onto the ground.

"Ball!" yelled out the other players, who were all looking on.

Unfortunately, all the Vaseline on Mace made Rosie's arms slip, and she accidentally pulled down his footy shorts.

OINK, OINK

When he stood up, Mace didn't realise his shorts were around his ankles. He had no idea why all the Nuggets players were rolling around on the ground laughing until he looked down and discovered he was somehow wearing *Peppa Pig* boxer shorts. Mace went bright red and shot a withering look at Chung, who avoided eye contact and started whistling innocently.

"Rosie will be the Nuggets' starting ruck-rover," declared Mr Scott.

This received a huge cheer from the players—as well as a few "oink, oink" sounds, which made Mace really, really mad.

15

A Tearful Ending

Fox was standing next to Lewis when the State Metro team arrived at the Diggers' ground. Their bus was large and sleek, and looked like it had been driven to Davinal from the future.

"It's so shiny it's like looking into the sun," said Lewis.

The players from the city stepped off the bus wearing really cool team tracksuits.

"They look more professional than ... professionals," said Lewis.

Last off the bus was the metropolitan coach, Barry Magro, who had his arm in a sling and his hand all bandaged up.

Mr Scott went straight over to him.

"What happened to your hand, Gigjam?" he asked.

A TEARFUL ENDING

"Um, I hurt it in a handball drill," said Barry.

The captain of the metro team, Marcus Prince, who had overheard this conversation, asked his coach later, "Hey, Mr Magro, how come that guy called you Gigjam?"

"Um it's a foreign word—German, actually," said Barry, thinking on the spot. "I think it means, um, 'The Terminator'."

"Cool, I'll get all the boys to start calling you Gigjam then," said Marcus.

"But—" Barry started to object but was distracted when he saw a kangaroo and a rabbit wearing red and gold capes. "I really need to get my eyes tested," he said.

Joey and Gary weren't the only supporters who had jumped on the Nuggets bandwagon. Hugo's sister Amanda was wearing a Nuggets jumper with her boyfriend Bruno's number on the back, and Snowy Davison and Matilda Wall were all decked out in red and gold, as were the parents, brothers and sisters of all the local players.

Inside the changing rooms the Nuggets players could not wait for the game to start. As usual, the Romana Roosters captain, Ed Gillies, was smiling. He looked over at Joey and Gary and said to Fox, "I can't believe you guys get to run out with them every week."

Mr Scott suddenly called for everyone's attention.

"Today you are representing your district, so you should all be very proud," he said. "This game isn't about winning or losing, it's about playing as a team and helping each other out."

"Yeah, come on, Nuggets!" yelled out a very pumped-up Strawbs O'Dwyer.

Strawbs' enthusiasm was infectious, and Fox and several other players yelled out "Come on!" as well.

"This is an incredibly talented group of footballers," continued Mr Scott, "but to do well today you have to work together. You have to want the ball more than the opposition, and even if you're exhausted, you have to push yourself to get over and shepherd a teammate or lay a tackle."

While Mr Scott was emphasising teamwork and everyone doing their best, over in the opposition changing rooms the metro coach was taking a different approach.

"I want you to crush the Nuggets like *gold dust*," said Barry Magro.

He was pretty happy with that line. He had been practising it in the mirror all week.

"Even though they are a hopeless collection of country bogans, I don't want you to go easy on them," he said.

"When you are 10 goals up halfway through the first quarter, I don't want anyone slacking off. I want you

A TEARFUL ENDING

to keep going hard to make sure we are 20 goals up by quarter-time," he thundered.

Five minutes later, both teams ran out onto the ground, although only the local side was accompanied by a kangaroo and a rabbit.

During the warm-up, Fox noticed the metro players were very well organised. They helped each other stretch, and then quickly took up positions to run through a series of short, sharp drills.

In contrast, the Nuggets players all did their own stretching, and their pre-game drills (apart from Cyril's fast handballs) were a rabble. Fox thought that he and his teammates must look, to the opposition, like stray cows wandering aimlessly around a paddock.

"Mmm, might need to email Cyril about a few more pre-game drills," he thought.

Fox overheard the metro captain saying to his coach, "Hey, check it out—they have four *girls* playing for them!"

Barry Magro started laughing uncontrollably.

"These guys are in for quite a surprise," thought Fox, shaking his head.

In fact the visiting team were in for a number of surprises, starting off in the ruck, where the Nuggets were able to take control from the first bounce. The athletic combination of Chris, Sammy and Strawbs was too much for the hapless metro ruckmen, who were both exhausted by the end of the first quarter.

In the forward line, Paige, Naso and Panos were way too fast and nimble for their opponents. The crowd went into a frenzy when Paige and Naso celebrated with a joint summersault after Panos slotted a goal from the boundary.

But the metro players were certainly very skilful and worked well together. Fox loved playing against such a good team, because it made him even more focused and determined. He lined up on the opposing captain and won possessions all over the ground. He and The Birdman both took absolute hangers in the first 10 minutes, much to the delight of the Nuggets supporters.

One area where the city team had an edge was with their tactics. They had sneaky strategies for kick outs and at **stoppages**, and they were very clever at **closing down space**. As a result they managed to kick a few easy goals.

"Mmm, might need to email Cyril about a few new tactics, too," thought Fox.

The other advantage the metro side had was that Mace was playing for himself and not the team. He refused to give the ball to a teammate in a better position, especially if that teammate was Fox, and because of that he **turned the ball over** several times, which allowed the metro boys to score a number of goals.

A TEARFUL ENDING

"Uslfshijutlftyagme!" said an unimpressed Mo.

"What did he say?" asked Mace.

"You don't want to know," said Rosie as she ran past.

Vince, who was taking his vice-captain duties very seriously, ran over to Mace and said, "Come on, Mace, look for the best option!"

Mace was furious, but the best response he could come up with was, "You're not the boss of me!"

Lewis, acting as the Nuggets' runner, was kept him very busy passing on messages from Mr Scott to Mace about being more of a team player.

But instead of listening to Lewis, Mace was abusive.

"What would you know, Rioli? You're the worst footballer in the school. Get lost!"

Mr Scott heard this and immediately called Mace off the ground and took him aside.

"Mace, I've taken you off firstly because you had a go at Lewis, which was completely unnecessary, and secondly because you keep playing as an individual," he said.

Mace rolled his eyes in disbelief.

"If you want to go back on," continued Mr Scott, "you'll have to apologise to Lewis and guarantee me you'll start playing for your teammates."

Mace stormed off and sat down on the bench with his back to the game and Mr Scott returned to coaching.

Throughout the first half Barry Magro was yelling out things to his team like, "You're falling down on the squeeze, so make sure you keep your structures!" and, "Set up the half-ground press, get them on the spread, and if you've got a plus-one make sure you use him!"

"What language is he speaking?" said Mr Scott, turning to Lewis.

When the half-time siren sounded, the scores were level.

| Nuggets | 7.12 (54) |
| State Metro | 8.6 (54) |

Even though the Nuggets weren't leading, they had clearly got on top towards the end of the quarter, especially after Mace had left the field. Simon had kicked the last two goals, Laser had started rebounding the footy out of the backline, and with the rucks dominating, Rosie, Chung, Ed Gillies and Fox were all **having a picnic** in the middle.

Mr Scott was confident his team would surge ahead in the second half, while Barry Magro had gone from being cocky to being alarmed. He could not believe the talent of country players, and once again his left eye started to twitch.

A TEARFUL ENDING

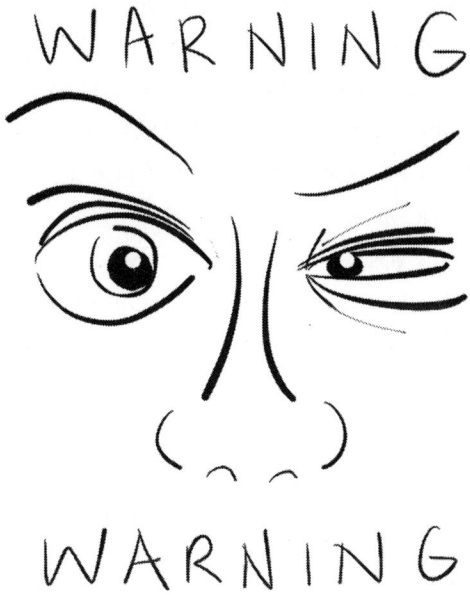

He walked over to Mr Scott as he was heading into the changing rooms, and casually suggested they call off the game.

"You know, it's quite hot today," he said, "and it is *only* a practice game after all—"

"I completely understand," said Mr Scott and a flicker of hope appeared in Barry's eyes, "if you want to *forfeit*—"

"Forfeit?! No way!" said Barry, and he stormed back into the changing rooms.

Just as Mr Scott predicted—and Barry Magro

feared—the Nuggets completely dominated the second half of the game.

Jacko, Sandy and Simon marked nearly everything that came into the forward line, and if the ball did hit the ground it was swooped on by Paige, Naso and Panos.

Down back, Mo, Bruno, Vince and The Birdman controlled the air. And as soon as one of them took a mark, Aslam, Roady or Lightning would flash by, take the handball, and send the footy deep into attack.

The Nuggets' lead had blown out to 12 goals midway through the last quarter, and everyone was kicking goals. Mo ran down the ground from full-back and from the centre of the ground kicked a massive torpedo punt that sailed through for a major.

"I have to get back on the ground and kick a goal," thought Mace.

He walked over to where Mr Scott and Lewis were standing and said, "All right, I'm sorry, Lewis, and I promise to play for the team, Mr Scott—can I go back on now?"

Mr Scott was not completely convinced by Mace's apology, mainly because of his lack of eye contact and also because he appeared to be crossing his fingers behind his back. However, he had been off the ground for nearly three quarters of the match, which was a pretty severe penalty.

"Okay, you can go back onto the right forward

A TEARFUL ENDING

flank," said Mr Scott. "But remember, I want you to play for the team."

"Yeah, yeah," said Mace as he dashed into position.

Two minutes later, Mace had a chance to show Mr Scott he had learned his lesson.

Rosie kicked the ball into the forward line and it bounced perfectly into Simon's arms in the goalsquare. All Mace had to do was shepherd for his teammate so that Simon could kick an easy goal.

But not only did Mace refuse to shepherd, he did not even call out to warn Simon that an opposition player was about to tackle him. As a result, Simon thought he was in the clear with no need to hurry, but as he went to kick his seventh goal, a speedy metro defender mowed him down.

Fox, who was standing more than 30 metres away, heard Simon's hamstring tear. The Nuggets full-forward went down holding the back of his right leg, screaming in agony.

Mr Scott had organised for the town's physiotherapist Justine Salmon to help out the Nuggets in case anyone was injured, and she and Lewis dashed onto the ground to help Simon off the field. Mr Scott looked on as Justine applied an ice pack to Simon's injured hamstring.

"Get Mace off now!" he said, turning to Lewis.

After being dragged, Mace sat stewing on the bench, again turning his back to the game.

His father rushed over to console him.

"On the plus side, it looks like the Diggers won't have a full-forward for the finals," said Mr Winter.

When Mr Scott heard this comment, he turned and started walking angrily towards Miles.

"Um Mace, I'd better go!" shrieked Miles, and he started running towards the exit gate.

When Mr Winter thought he was a safe distance away, he stopped and turned to face Mr Scott.

"I'm not scared of you!" he called out.

Suddenly Miles heard a thumping sound that seemed to be getting closer and closer. He spun around just in time to see Joey bounding straight for him.

A TEARFUL ENDING

"Ahhhhhhhhhhhhhhhhhhhh!" he screamed and bolted for his car.

The Nuggets supporters all cheered, and Joey hopped back towards them, stopped and appeared to take a small bow.

The siren sounded to end the game and Mr Scott immediately walked over to where Barry Magro was standing.

"Oh great," thought Barry, "he's coming over to gloat."

But instead Mr Scott said, "Thanks very much for the game—you've got some excellent players in your team."

Barry was speechless. If the roles were reversed he would have been rubbing the other coach's nose in it.

"It's amazing how much talent there is in our local competition," continued Mr Scott. "The win today has got nothing to do with me—I'd hate to think how good they'd be with an experienced coach like yourself looking after them. Have a safe trip back to town, Barry."

Mr Scott held out his hand. Barry looked at it, then shook it awkwardly with his left hand and said, "Thanks Greg, that means a lot to me."

Barry wasn't sure what he appreciated more, the kind words or the fact that Mr Scott had called him Barry and not Gigjam.

"Maybe no one will ever call me Gigjam again?" he thought hopefully.

"Hey Gigjam!" called out Marcus Prince. "The bus driver wanted me to remind you that we're leaving in half an hour."

"Or maybe they will," sighed Barry.

The first thing Fox did back in the changing rooms was check to see if Simon was okay. He was still icing his hammy, and Fox offered to help in any way he could. He felt very sorry for Simon, but he knew his Diggers teammate would do everything he could to overcome his injury. Fox also remembered what Cyril had said in his email to Mr Scott—"If one soldier goes down, there's always another one to take their place."

A number of Diggers had played at full-forward this season, and while none of them were as good as Simon, at least they had some experience in that position.

Fox then went around congratulating his teammates for playing such a super game. He noticed that Vince was doing this as well, and had to admit that he had been an excellent vice-captain for the Nuggets.

Fox had started chatting to Paige about a spectacular dribble goal she had kicked in the third quarter, when he noticed that Mo was sitting by himself. Fox thought he looked sad, which was unusual as Mo normally had a big grin on his face.

A TEARFUL ENDING

Fox signalled for Paige to join him and wandered over to talk to the star full-back.

"Hey Mo, brilliant game today," said Fox

"Anxewtoo."

Fox could tell something was wrong. "What's going on, Mo?"

Mo explained (and Paige translated) that there had been some more bad news on the farm. Somehow their measly water supply had been poisoned, and now they would have to pay someone to cart water to the farm—something they could not afford.

"Wirdefgonnahaftaselna," said Mo.

Fox didn't have to ask Paige to translate this, the look in Mo's eye told him exactly what he'd said— "We are definitely going to have to sell the farm now."

16

'It's All 'Bout that Mace'

After the game Mr Swift was giving a number of the players a lift home in his kombi. The mood in the van was so gloomy that if he hadn't been at the game, Mr Swift would have assumed the Nuggets had lost.

A dejected Simon was in the very back with his leg up on the seat and an ice pack strapped around hamstring. Mo Officer looked just as sad as he sat staring out the window without speaking—or even mumbling—a word. So when a song by Meghan Trainor came on the radio, Mr Swift looked at Fox in the rear-view mirror, turned up the volume and started to sing along. As always, he made up his own lyrics:

Because you know it's all about that Mace
'Bout that Mace, he's trouble

'IT'S ALL 'BOUT THAT MACE'

It's all 'bout that Mace, 'bout that Mace, he's trouble
It's all 'bout that Mace, 'bout that Mace, he's trouble
It's all 'bout that Mace, 'bout that Mace
Yeah it's pretty clear, he don't have no clue
'Cause he don't pass the ball, like he's supposed to do
'Cause he don't go "Vroom, Vroom" when all the boys chase
He gets caught with the ball, in all the wrong places
I see the metro team, worrying non-stop
They know that Simon's unreal
No full-back can make him stop
If you got two white flags, just raise 'em up
'Cause every kick he do is perfect
Like cream he rises to the top

Simon raised his hand to thank Mr Swift and everyone laughed as Fox's dad continued with his song.

Yeah, Mo's momma she told him don't worry about your thighs
She says thighs like that let you kick footys way out of sight
You know Mo won't play no selfish, silly-dumb, baby games
But that's what Mace is into
So Mr Scott says, "Move along"
Because you know it's all about that Mace

'Bout that Mace, he's trouble
It's all 'bout that Mace, 'bout that Mace, he's trouble
It's all 'bout that Mace, 'bout that Mace, he's trouble
It's all 'bout that Mace, 'bout that Mace
I'm taking Mace off the footy track
Go ahead and take him off through the witches' hats
And I'm saying you're never coming back

By now everyone knew the words, so they all joined in for the chorus.

So Mr Scott says, "Move along"
Because you know it's all about that Mace
'Bout that Mace, he's trouble
It's all 'bout that Mace, 'bout that Mace, he's trouble
It's all 'bout that Mace, 'bout that Mace, he's trouble
It's all 'bout that Mace, 'bout that Mace

They sang so loudly that Fox was worried the roof of the kombi would be blown off.

At the end of the song everyone burst out laughing. It was fantastic to see Simon and Mo smiling again, and Fox really hoped their luck would change soon.

"Fox are you going to have a shower?" asked his mother.

She never understood Fox and Chase's reluctance to have a shower as soon as they arrived home from footy.

'IT'S ALL 'BOUT THAT MACE'

"Yes, Mum, but I have to send an email first."

"It must be a pretty important email if it can't wait for you to get out of your stinky football gear."

"It is," said Fox as he began typing.

Hi Cyril,

Hope you are well. The combined team from our league beat the State Metro under-14s, which was pretty cool. The only problem is that Simon tore his hamstring really badly and there is only about a month before the finals start. I know you had hamstring problems in the past, so do you have any tips or advice for him so he can recover in time?

Thanks heaps,
Fox Swift.

PS Also, during the match against the metro team, I noticed they used some really good tactics, especially at the kick-ins, boundary throw-ins and ball-ups. In terms of tactics, we don't really have—well, any! Could you please email some ideas to Mr Scott so that can pass them on to Hugo, who is coaching the under-11s?

"Now can you have a shower?" said Mrs Swift.

"Sure—oh, hang on, I think I've a got a reply coming through."

Hi Fox,

Sorry to hear about Simon's injury. Tell him not to be too down—I know exactly how he's feeling. If he looks after his injury and does all his rehab I'm sure he will be able play in the finals, but make sure he sees a physio ASAP. I'll also send through a list of all the exercises I did to get my hammies sorted, and Simon can talk these through with the physio.

All the best,
Cyril

PS Great win against the State Metro under-14s—I've met Barry Magro and I'll bet old Gigjam wasn't happy!

PPS Tactics can make a big difference—I will email some through to Greg ASAP.

PPPS It's really cool that Hugo is coaching!

Two days later Simon had an appointment with Justine Salmon at her clinic, Hands-on Physiotherapy. As he sat nervously in the waiting room, he re-read the printout of Cyril's exercises and tips to stop himself from worrying about the finals.

Justine called Simon into her office and examined him. She then explained that he had a serious tear in his hamstring.

"Will I be able to play in the finals in a month's time?" he asked.

Justine paused before answering. She didn't want to give her patient any false hope, but she also didn't want to crush his dreams.

"It's possible," she said. "If you do all the exercises I set you, and don't have any setbacks, then you have a chance."

"Don't worry, I'll definitely do everything you tell me," said Simon, smiling with relief.

Justine read the email Cyril had sent through and told Simon it was an excellent summary of what she would like him to do. Then she demonstrated each of the exercises and drew little diagrams for him to take home, in case he forgot how to do them properly.

"I'll see you again in a week and we can see how you are progressing," said Justine. The determined look in Simon's eye told her that he was going to do everything in his power to fix his hamstring by the finals. She just hoped that would be enough.

"Hey Chase, you want a kick of the footy?" asked Fox.

"No can do," replied Chase.

Fox was in shock. Chase had never said no to a kick of the footy before. Ever.

"Huh?"

"Jimmy, Gregor and I are filling in for Simon at the refugee centre," explained Chase.

Every week for the past year Simon had been running a fitness class for all the children at the refugee centre. He would make them jog on the spot, do push-ups, sit-ups, squats, **burpees** and star jumps for a solid half an hour—and the kids loved it!

Simon's hamstring injury meant he wasn't able to take the class, so Chase, Jimmy and their giant friend, Gregor 'The Burpinator' Ivanisovich, had offered to fill in for him.

Fox looked at his brother and smiled. "Chase is really starting to grow up," he thought to himself.

'IT'S ALL 'BOUT THAT MACE'

The kids at the centre had a ball with their three new instructors. It was half an hour of laughing as much as exercise—which Chase figured meant their stomach muscles got twice the workout.

The funniest moment came when Chase asked Gregor to show the kids how to do burpees, and Gregor opened his mouth and burped out the letter 'E' three times. The children rolled around on the ground in stitches.

After the workout was finished, Gregor showed the kids how to burp the alphabet. It was the funniest thing they had ever seen.

They were so impressed that the next day they were all burping the alphabet, too. Initially their parents were upset, but then they realised it was the first time their children had taken an interest in learning the alphabet, so they ended up burping along as well.

Mr Grinter's droning voice could make even the most interesting biology lesson sound boring.

" ... As everyone knows, when ostriches are frightened they like to bury their heads in the sand—"

Straight away two hands shot up into the air—Hugo's and Chung's.

"Oh here we go," thought Mr Grinter.

So far this month Hugo and Chung had corrected him when he had said camels store water in their humps; goldfish only have a three-second memory; dogs only see in black and white; and bats are blind. Wrong, wrong, wrong, wrong.

Sally Renton had kindly made a note of each of these mistakes, all of which Mr Grinter was sure had been passed on to her father.

"I think it's your turn, Chung," said Hugo politely.

"Thanks, Hugo," said Chung. "Mr Grinter, ostriches don't actually bury their heads in the sand—they just press their necks to the ground, so their enemies find them harder to see."

Just as Sally Renton started to make a note in her pad, her father burst into the room.

"Uh oh, a visit from the principal!" thought Mr

Grinter. "This can't be good."

Mr Renton stood at the front of the class and said a word he had never used before when talking to Mr Grinter, "Congratulations!"

"Um, thanks," said Mr Grinter. "Congratulations for … ?"

"For your class winning the competition," replied the principal.

"The competition?"

"For the all expenses paid trip to the city to visit the Synchrotron," said Mr Renton, handing over a large envelope containing all the details.

"The Sinka-what?" thought Mr Grinter.

"So well done," said Mr Renton. "Keep up the good work, Morgan."

Hugo and Chung gave each other a sneaky high five as Mr Renton left the classroom. They had secretly entered a school science competition on behalf of the class a few months ago, and were thrilled to discover they had won.

Mr Grinter turned to the class. He was totally confused, so he did what he always did in these situations— ask the class a question pretending he already knew the answer.

"So, who here knows what a, um, Sink-a-tron thingy is?"

Three hands shot up in the air. Two of them belonged

to Hugo and Chung, so Mr Grinter went for the third option.

"Yes, Vince?"

"Vince?" thought Fox.

The whole class turned around to stare at Vince. Mace, who sitting next to him, muttered, "This'll be good!"

"Um, it's a scientific research facility that produces beams of light that examine the atomic and molecular detail of a wide range of materials," said Vince.

There was silence. Everyone was stunned.

"What?" asked Mr Grinter.

"It's like a gigantic laboratory," said Vince.

"That's right," said Mr Grinter. "A gigantic laboratory."

Vince looked at Mace and said, "We're going to the Synchrotron—this is so cool."

"How come?" sneered Mace.

"Um, 'coz, you know, like, we get out of class for a whole day," said Vince.

Mace weighed up this answer, and eventually nodded at Vince.

"Good call—maybe you're not so dumb after all."

Vince was very relieved that Mace believed his little fib. He was actually just as excited about visiting the Synchrotron as Hugo and Chung.

Two weeks earlier, Mr Grinter had announced that

three kids in the class had achieved a perfect score on a science test. Predictably, he handed back two of these tests to Hugo and Chung. He then walked over to Vince's desk and placed his test in front of him.

Vince smiled proudly, but Mr Grinter frowned and said, "You've got a detention for cheating!"

Mace was furious with Vince—not because he had cheated, but because he hadn't given him the answers, too.

"Vince, you idiot!" he whispered. "You never get 100 per cent when you're cheating. Always throw in a couple of mistakes so no one will suspect you ... Or, in your case, throw in a *lot* of mistakes!"

What nobody realised was that Vince hadn't cheated.

17

Lab Rat

The bus taking Fox's class to the Synchrotron was due to leave the school at 7am sharp.

The bus driver was a grumpy old man called 'Gibbo'. He had bushy eyebrows and seemed to have more hair growing out of his nose and ears than from the top of his head. He was angry because it was now a quarter past seven and the bus couldn't leave because Mr Grinter still hadn't arrived. Gibbo expected students to be late, but not the teacher.

Fox looked out the bus window while they waited and raised his eyebrows in amazement when he saw that an entire wall of the school's administration building was now missing. Part of the roof had also been removed, and multi-coloured plastic coverings were flapping in the wind.

"Wow, Miss Carey *really* hates termites," he said to himself.

Fox's thoughts were interrupted by the arrival of a sweaty Mr Grinter.

"Sorry I'm late," he said as he boarded the bus. "A burglar broke into my home. Luckily, he didn't take anything, but he must have turned off my alarm clock. The important thing is that I'm okay."

All the students laughed at this unbelievable excuse, except for Sally Renton, who shook her head and started scribbling wildly on her pad.

Mr Grinter tried to seize back control.

"I expect you to all behave on this bus trip. Rest assured I will be keeping a very close eye on each and every one of you," he said sternly.

He then sat down and was sound asleep and snoring before they were even at the sign that said, "You are leaving Davinal".

The bus trip was pretty uneventful, apart from Mace using a peashooter to fire spit-covered balls of paper at his classmates.

He was lining up the back of Fox's head when Vince accidentally bumped him, and instead of blowing out, Mace sucked in and nearly choked when the small paper ball became stuck in his throat.

When the bus arrived at the Synchrotron Mr Grinter was still sound asleep. Gibbo shook his shoulder to wake him.

"Ahhhhhh! You've drooled all over my seat!" complained the bus driver.

The students got down off the bus and Fox stared at the gigantic round building in front of them. The sign read "Australian Synchrotron".

"Wow!" said Lewis. "It's even bigger than Mace's ego!"

A man in a white coat walked over and gave them a friendly greeting.

"Hi, I'm Professor Speele. And by scientific deduction, you must be the kids from Davinal. I'll be taking you on a tour of the Synchrotron today."

Fox looked over at Hugo, who was so excited he was almost jogging on the spot.

"The Synchrotron is kind of like a super-dooper x-ray machine—an x-ray machine the size of the MCG," said their tour guide.

"Maybe I should have brought my footy," thought Fox.

"Now before I take you on the tour, I'm going to check your level of scientific understanding by telling you a joke," said Professor Speele.

Fox had never managed to understand any of Hugo's science jokes, but he was hoping the professor's one might be a little easier to follow.

"Okay, so there were two atoms, and one atom says to the other atom, 'Hey I lost an electron!' and the other atom says, 'Are you *positive*?'"

Hugo, Chung and Vince burst out laughing, while

the rest of the class, including Mr Grinter, stared blankly at the professor.

"Okay, so we've got three smart ones here," said the professor.

Mace pointed at Vince and laughed, "Ha! As if this guy got the joke—he's the dumbest in the class."

"I'm sure that's not the case," said Professor Speele, and then he turned to Vince. "Would you like to explain the joke to rest of the class?" he asked kindly.

"Um," said Vince.

"I told you!" said Mace.

But Vince ignored Mace and surprised everyone by saying, "If an atom gains or loses an electron it's no longer neutral and it becomes an ion. If it gains an electron, which is negative, it becomes a negative ion, but if it loses an electron, like in your joke, it becomes a positive ion. That's why the other atom says, 'Are you positive?'"

"Very good," said Professor Speele. "What's your name?"

"Vince Brogan."

"Brogan? You're not related to Professor Albert Brogan, are you?"

"Yeah, he's my uncle."

Hugo and Chung turned to each other and raised their eyebrows in disbelief. Professor Albert Brogan was one of the most famous scientists in the country, and even though Vince had the same surname, they had never made the connection because—well, because Vince was Vince.

Fox found the tour really interesting, mainly because Professor Speele was a fantastic teacher—both funny and smart.

"Kind of the opposite of Mr Grinter," thought Fox.

I'VE GOT MY ION YOU

Professor Speele explained that more than 4000 people did experiments at the Synchrotron each year. Some were medical scientists trying to discover new drugs to help sick people; some were experts from mining companies trying to find out what minerals lay beneath the earth. And others came from art galleries wanting to work out where certain paintings had came from or whether another masterpiece lay underneath.

While they were walking around the Synchrotron and its massive twisting pipes, Hugo and Chung went over to talk to Vince.

"Professor Albert Brogan is your uncle?" said Hugo.

"Yep!" said Vince proudly.

"No way!" said Chung. "He's like the most intelligent professor in Australia—he's even worked on the **Hadron Collider**."

"I know, it's really cool," said Vince. "I was talking to him about that on the phone the other day—"

"No way known!" said Hugo.

"Do you think we could meet your uncle one day?" asked Chung.

"I don't see why not," said Vince.

"Cool!" said Hugo. "Hey, I've got another atom gag for you! Why should you never trust an atom? Because they make up everything!"

Mace looked across and saw Vince laughing with Hugo and Chung and was furious. "Time to break up the nerd conference," he said to himself.

As he walked over, he heard Chung saying, "... Yeah we should definitely do a Bragg Diffraction Experiment one weekend."

"Cool!" said Vince

"Cool?! The Bag Deflection Experiment is *so* lame!" sneered Mace, pretending he understood what they were talking about.

"Bag Deflection?" said Vince as Hugo and Chung started laughing. "Um, no, Mace, it's the *Bragg Diffraction* Experiment. It was named after an English father and son team of physicists, Sir W.H. and Sir W.L. Bragg. They both won Nobel Prizes. Actually, my uncle told me a funny story about these guys. They were in their laboratory one night, and—"

"You're acting really weird, Vince. You've got to stop hanging out with these losers," said Mace, dragging Vince away.

As he was being led off, Vince mouthed, "Sorry!" to Hugo and Chung.

There were a number of small rooms at the Synchrotron where scientists would conduct their experiments and check their results. Fox, who had wandered away from the group, peered through a window into one of these rooms and froze. He rubbed his eyes to make sure he wasn't seeing things.

On the other side of the glass was Miles Winter. He was holding what appeared to be a small leaf, which he handed over to a man in a white coat, who in turn placed it into a machine and looked through what appeared to be a microscope. Mr Winter seemed very happy, and laughed as he gave the scientist an enthusiastic slap on the back.

Fox didn't have a clue why Mr Winter was there, but he thought of a phrase his dad always used when something was suspicious: "I smell a rat."

On the bus trip home, Fox leaned across the aisle and said to Hugo, "I saw Mr Winter at the Synchrotron."

"What?" said Hugo in surprise.

As Fox explained exactly what he had witnessed, Hugo pulled out his pad and began taking notes.

"Mmm a leaf, you say? That's interesting. *Very* interesting," said Hugo.

18

Cunning Like a Dingo

The next Sunday, Fox and his friends went around to the Officers' farm to help out.

The Diggers players did a variety of farm chores in the morning, including feeding Johnny and Cash, collecting firewood and throwing hay to the sheep from the back of the ute.

Back in the Officers' homestead over lunch, they chatted non-stop about the great win they'd had over the Morgan Bridge Magpies the day before.

"How good was it when Mr Scott moved Mo to full-forward and he kicked four goals?" said Hugo.

"Ijuzgtlukee," said Mo modestly.

"It wasn't luck, Mo," said Paige.

"And what about Rosie's blind turn just before half-time? I swear that Morgan Bridge player still doesn't know where she went," said Lewis.

"And Laser's **give and go** to Chung in the third quarter was brilliant," said Rosie.

"Do you kids ever talk about anything other than football?" asked Mrs Officer.

"Have you been talking to my mother?" said Fox.

Just then the phone rang. Mr Officer slowly rose from his chair and walked over and picked up the receiver. Fox noticed that a worried look had appeared on the farmer's tanned face.

"Who was it, dear?" asked Mrs Officer when her husband returned to the table.

"Dunnohesedcuplashipgitcotinfensonsuthnpadok," said Mr Officer as he headed out the door.

Mrs Officer saw the confused look on Fox's face and said, "Mr Officer didn't catch the name of the caller, but whoever it was said that a small number of sheep had become caught in a fence in a southern paddock."

Everyone bolted out the door after Mr Officer and jumped into the back of the ute. They drove all the way over to the far southern paddock, but there didn't appear to be any sheep stuck in the fence.

Mr Officer stopped the ute, jumped out and scratched his head.

"Mustagtowtbimselvs," he said.

"The sheep must have been able to extract themselves

from the fence on their own," whispered Paige.

Fox looked around and noticed something out of the corner of his eye.

"Mr Officer, what's that?" he asked pointing into the distance.

A small cloud of smoke hovered above a paddock on the other side of the farm.

"Fiyah!" yelled Mr Officer.

"Fire!" whispered Paige.

"I got that one," said Fox.

They all jumped back into the ute, and Mr Officer quickly drove over to a big shed and grabbed a pump, a large hose and a pile of neatly stacked buckets. They then raced around to where the fire had started. Fortunately there was a dam in the paddock very close to the fire. Normally it would have been empty, but just that morning the water carting company had come and filled it up.

Mr Officer and Mo quickly set up the pump and soon the big black rubber hose was spouting water into the belly of the fire. Meanwhile, Fox, Paige, Rosie, Hugo, Lewis, Chung and Aslam formed a chain gang, filling up buckets of water and dumping them on little spot fires before they could grow into giant walls of flame.

They battled the fire for at least half an hour before the fire brigade arrived and took control of the situation.

Everyone was completely exhausted and covered from head to toe in soot. The Diggers players all lay down next to the now empty dam, while Mo went around thanking them for their help.

After the fire was completely extinguished Harry Mackay, the fire chief, walked over to Mr Officer and said, "Sorry we took so long to get here, mate. We were called out to another fire on the other side of Davinal, but it turned out to be a false alarm."

Fox saw Hugo frown, pull out his pen and pad and make a couple of notes, before jumping up and wandering around the paddock sniffing the air. All of a sudden he stopped, sniffed the air again, and made another entry in his pad.

Mrs Officer arrived with a giant container of homemade lemonade and a basket filled with Anzac biscuits, and went around offering them to everyone who had helped put out the fire. She looked at the dam and walked over to Mr Officer.

"Our water's all gone," she said.

"Leecefardidnbundwn," said Mr Officer

"Yes, the farm didn't burn down," said Mrs Officer, "but the children could have been hurt."

Mr Officer nodded slowly and then stared at the ground.

"Maybe it will be okay," said Mrs Officer, trying to cheer up her husband. "I'll make an appointment with

Mr Shloogal at the bank and see if he can give us some more time."

The next day Mr and Mrs Officer left Mo in the ute outside the bank while they went inside to have their meeting with Mr Shloogal.

When they were all inside his office, Mr Shloogal shook his head, took off his glasses and started cleaning them with his handkerchief.

"I'd *really* like to help you out, Mr and Mrs Officer," said Mr Shloogal, "but unfortunately the decision has already been made by others."

"Others?" said Mrs Officer.

The banker shrugged his shoulders and pointed at the ceiling.

Mrs Officer looked at him strangely. "You mean … God?" she asked.

"No, no, I mean my manager. Although, in a way, he is kind of like a god."

"Does your manager work upstairs?" asked a confused Mrs Officer.

"No, in the city."

"Then why did you point up?"

"Because my boss is above me on the company organisational chart … Look, it's just something we say in banking, okay?"

"If you could just give us an extra month—"

Mr Shloogal raised his hand, cutting off Mrs Officer before she could finish her sentence. He then held up a piece of paper and said, "According to the contract that you and your husband signed, you have to pay the bank $100,000 within the next three weeks, or else—"

"Or else you'll take our farm," said Mrs Officer.

"Well … there is one other option," said Mr Shloogal. "If you sign over your farm to Selim Properties, they have generously offered to pay off all the money you owe."

"Wdblftwitnuthin!" mumbled Mr Officer.

"Huh?" said Mr Shloogal

"Unfortunately that would mean we'd be left without any financial assets," translated Mrs Officer.

"But you wouldn't owe anyone anything," said Mr Shloogal soothingly.

"Allnoizfarmin,"

"Mr Officer's skills are primarily related to running a farm, and he wouldn't know what else to do."

"Ltsthinabowtit,"

"If you could give us a bit of time to contemplate our options that would be much appreciated."

"Unfortunately I can only give you the three weeks," said Mr Shloogal.

"Yes, because of—" Mrs Officer said sarcastically, pointing upwards.

Mo watched his parents as they came out of the bank and walked back towards to the ute. He had never seen them looking so down.

In the last home and away game of the year, Fox watched on as Chase led out the Diggers under-11s in their match against the Firbush Fever.

Before the start of the game, Lewis walked around the players as they stretched, busily passing on Hugo's secret coaching tips.

Chase played a brilliant first quarter and Fox was very proud of his little brother. He took a screamer, snapped a brilliant left-foot goal from the boundary, and, most importantly, he constantly brought his teammates into the game with his **creative handballs**.

By quarter-time the Diggers were up by 35 points. Mr Percy yawned continuously as he spoke to the players during the break.

"Firbush are as useless as the checkout chick who served me in the local supermarket last week. Just because I had *slightly* more than 12 items in my *two* trolleys, she wanted me to move to a different queue. Well, I said to her, 'Listen here, Missy—'"

Chase rolled his eyes and thought, "We are so lucky to have Hugo!"

As Mr Percy continued his rant about the declining standards of customer service in Davinal, Hugo quietly made his way around the group whispering advice and positional changes.

Mr Percy was so bored in the second quarter he quietly slipped away to the changing rooms and crawled under a table for a snooze. With the official Diggers coach absent, Hugo was able to call out his instructions and positional moves from the boundary. The players loved it.

One ingenious move he made was to put Adesh Gupta to centre half-forward. Adesh quickly showed he was not only capable of spoiling opposition full-forwards, but could also take strong marks and kick goals. The highlight of the half occurred after he kicked his third goal, when he performed a couple of quick Bollywood dance moves. The supporters from both teams went wild.

At half-time Mini and Soobs were chatting to each other as they walked back into the changing rooms.

"Hugo is the best coach ever!" said Soobs.

"I know, and Mr Percy doesn't suspect a thing!" said Mini.

"Yep, he's completely clueless," said Soobs, giving Mini a high five.

Mr Percy, who had just woken up, managed to overhear the girls' conversation.

"Clueless, am I?" he said, bursting out from underneath the table.

Unfortunately for Mr Percy, he bumped his head on the edge of the table on the way out, which kind of answered his own question.

"Ouch!" he said.

"Were you sleeping under the table?" asked Chase.

"No," lied Mr Percy. "I was setting a trap. And you nincompoops fell for it."

"Nincompoops?" said Chase. "What's a nincompoop?"

Mr Percy ignored the question and said, "Now which one of you is Hugo?"

"How could you not know who I am?" said Hugo. "You coached me for three games in the under-12s and I was the only one in the whole league who wore a bodysuit!"

"Whatevs," said Mr Percy. "All I know is that you are banned from coming anywhere near my under-11s team for the rest of the season."

All the players groaned and Joey, who had snuck into the rooms, shook her head and made a "tch, tch" sound.

"And that stupid kangaroo is banned, too!" screamed Mr Percy.

"What?" said Chase

"Don't argue with me, Dingo!" said the coach

"But this isn't fair—hey, don't call me Dingo!"

"Okay Dingo, that's it! You're on the bench for the rest of the game."

"No way!" said Jimmy, leaping to Chase's defence.

"You're off, too, whatever your name is."

"That's ridiculous!" said JT.

"And you!"

"Man, you are one uptight dude," said Zebidiah Fontaine.

"And you!"

In the second half the Diggers had only 14 players on the field, and to make matters worse Mr Percy played everyone out of position. Despite having been 12 goals up at half-time, the team eventually lost to the bottom-placed Fever by two points.

When Mr Percy called the team in at the end of the game, Chase expected him to apologise, but all the coach said before stomping off to his car was, "Serves you losers right! Laters."

On Monday after school, Mr Percy was at home putting some wax on his pencil-thin moustache when his doorbell rang.

"Oooh that must be the new 'I heart Chickpeas' T-shirt I ordered online," he thought.

He raced over and opened the door of his flat, then

stepped back in alarm. The entire Davinal Diggers under-11s team stood before him with their arms crossed and angry expressions on their faces. Mr Percy also noticed that in among the group of children was a fairly hostile-looking kangaroo.

Chase stood in front of his teammates and said, "Mr Percy, we need to talk."

"No we don't," said the world's worst coach. "My decision is final and when Percival Percy makes up his mind he doesn't change it."

"Your name is *Percival* Percy?" said Chase, raising his eyebrows in disbelief.

"I know! Cool, isn't it?"

"Um … Listen, Mr Percy, we heard you on the phone at the start of the season saying you hate kids, you hate footy, and the only reason you took on the coaching job was to help you get a job in the city," said Chase.

"That's true, but who cares?"

"Well just suppose we ring up Triple D FM and tell Shazza and Bazza that it's really been Hugo and not you who has been coaching us all year?"

"So what?"

"Once everyone knows you weren't the real coach you won't be able to say you 'helped the community' on any of your job applications."

A couple of beads of sweat appeared on Mr Percy's forehead as he began to understand the point Chase was making.

"Then you won't get a job in the city and you'll be stuck in Davinal with us—um, what did you call us again … 'mountain-bullies'?"

"I said hillbillies!"

"Whatevs," said Chase, who was now in total control.

Mr Percy thought about this for a while, and then an extremely fake smile appeared on his face.

"Um, I *may* have been a little hasty before. How about we just go back to the way we were doing things before?"

Chase shook his head.

"No. How about from now on Hugo takes us for training instead of you?"

"Fine!" snapped Mr Percy. "I hate taking training anyway."

"And from now on, Hugo talks to us during the

quarter-time, half-time and three-quarter time breaks."

"I don't care."

"And Joey leads us out onto the field during the finals—"

"Okay, okay! You win, Dingo! Do whatever you want. The only thing I care about is being in the photo at the end of the season so I can prove I was the coach."

Mr Percy slammed the door shut and Chase turned to his teammates, who all started clapping and cheering.

"Way to go, Dingo!" yelled out Jimmy.

"Hey, don't call me Dingo!" said Chase.

"We promise we won't," said Jimmy. "Dingo! Dingo! Dingo! Dingo!"

Chase shook his head and smiled as the rest of the Diggers joined in Jimmy's chant.

stop calling me DINGO!

19

A Digger Departs

Simon Phillips had never been so nervous in all his life.

Mr Scott had told him he could only play in the first final against the Stonewarren Stingrays if his physiotherapist gave him the all-clear.

Simon gently knocked on the orange-coloured door of his physio's office and crossed his fingers.

"Come in!" said Justine Salmon.

He took a deep breath, turned the doorknob and walked in.

"Hi Simon," said Justine, smiling warmly. "How's the hammy feeling?"

"Um pretty good, I think."

"How about we go straight into doing a few tests?"

After checking his flexibility with a few stretches,

Justine made Simon do a series of exercises, including regular squats, one-legged squats, jumping lunges and burpees.

SIMON DOES A BURPEE

"It's important to see how the hamstring holds up when you're fatigued," explained Justine.

"Well, you're doing a good job of fatiguing me!" puffed Simon after his 50th burpee.

"You're doing great, Simon—so far. Now let's head outside and do a few more tests."

There was a park across the road from Justine's office, and they headed there with a bag full of footballs and several witches' hats.

Justine started the outdoor testing by asking Simon to do some straight line run throughs—at half pace, then three-quarter pace, then full pace.

"How are you feeling?"

"Fine," said Simon.

"Okay, let's make this next test a little more difficult."

Justine set up two of the orange cones about five metres apart and instructed Simon to run back and forth between them 10 times. Each time he had to bend down to touch the base of a cone before quickly turning and running back to the other one. He also did this exercise at half pace, three-quarter pace and finally at top speed.

"You okay?" asked Justine.

Simon gave her the thumbs up.

"Excellent! Now there's one final test to go," she said, taking six footballs out of the bag and laying them on the ground.

"I want you to run 20 metres to the ball, bend down, pick it up and kick the footy in between those two trees in front of you. You'll kick three times with your right foot and three times with your left foot—got it?"

Simon nodded. He knew that if his hamstring managed to stand up during this final test, he would be playing against the Stingrays on Saturday.

"Come on!" he said to himself.

"And I need you to do all six of these flat out," said Justine.

Simon did exactly as he was told. The first five times he went flat out, scooped up the ball and produced a deadly accurate kick in between the two trees.

"Just one more," said Justine as he jogged back into position.

Simon shut his eyes and whispered to his hamstring, "Please don't let me down now!"

He took off and, when he hit top speed, swooped on the ball and drilled a perfect 40-metre drop punt between the trees.

"Yesssss!" yelled Simon and Justine at the same time.

The Diggers full-forward was not sure which of them was happier.

"I didn't know if I'd get through that," he confessed.

"I thought you would," said Justine. "Of all the patients I've ever had, and that includes a few AFL players, none have worked as hard as you to overcome an injury."

"So can I tell Mr Scott I can play?"

"Not quite. The last thing you need to do is see how you pull up in the morning. If you wake up and your hamstring feels completely okay, then you can ring Mr Scott and tell him you are cleared for the finals."

When Simon woke up the next morning his thoughts immediately turned to his right hamstring. He tried to work out if he felt any pains or aches by carefully shifting onto his side. Nothing. He slowly lowered his feet over the side of his bed until they hit the floor. Nothing. He gently stood up and started walking. Nothing—absolutely no pain at all.

"Woohoo!" he yelled as he sprinted down the hallway. Mr Scott's number was sitting by the phone in readiness for the call and he quickly punched in the numbers.

"Mr Scott, Mr Scott! I can play!"

There was a pause at the other end of the phone and then a croaky voice replied, "That's great, Simon—um, do you have any idea what time it is?"

Simon squinted at the clock in the kitchen.

"It's um … 5.17am—oops! Sorry, Mr Scott."

"No worries, Simon, I'm really glad you can play tomorrow. See you at the ground."

If Simon thought that conversation with his coach was going to be his most exciting call for the day, he was wrong. Just before he sat down for dinner that night, the phone rang. His mum answered it then turned to Simon with a smile. "It's for you," she said.

Simon took the receiver with a surprised look on his face. He wasn't expecting a call from anyone!

"Hello, Simon speaking."

"Hi Simon, it's Cyril—"

"Cyril, as in *Cyril Rioli* Cyril?" stammered Simon.

"Yep, I just wanted to see how you were doing with your hammy."

"I passed the fitness test yesterday!"

"That's fantastic! I went through exactly the same thing with the Hawks, and the important thing to do is push the injury out of your mind as much as you can and just focus on the ball and doing as many team things as you can."

Simon's foot started tapping with excitement as he listened carefully the Hawthorn champ's advice.

"No one's going to expect you to kick 10 goals in your first game back. All you have to do is the **one-percenters**. Chase your opponent, don't let the ball come out of the forward line too easily, and when you have a chance to kick a goal make the most of it."

By the end of the phone call Simon was feeling so much better. Cyril's hamstring injury had been much worse than his, and yet he had managed to play well in the biggest game of the season, the 2014 AFL Grand Final. That night, the Diggers full-forward went to sleep with a big smile on his face.

O n the Saturday morning of the first final, Fox walked into the Diggers' changing rooms with Chase. While his brother changed into his footy gear, Fox picked up a copy of the *Record*.

He turned to the page with the competition ladder, and smiled with pride.

A DIGGER DEPARTS

	P	W	L	Pts	%
Davinal Diggers	11	11	0	44	287
Stonewarren Stingrays	11	9	2	36	181
Davinal Drongos	11	9	2	36	125
Romana Roosters	11	8	3	32	160
Ballymore Bears	11	8	3	32	138
Shepton Sharks	11	6	5	24	128
Colbran Cockatoos	11	5	6	20	114
Tennant Hill Tigers	11	4	7	16	79
Gregtown Goannas	11	3	8	12	55
Firbush Fever	11	2	9	8	43
Linmore Leopards	11	1	10	4	42
Morgan Bridge Magpies	11	0	11	0	25

The Diggers had finished the home and away season undefeated, but Fox knew that once the finals began it was like they were starting from scratch.

He then flicked over to the On This Day page, where as usual his coach was mentioned.

> On this day 40 years ago ... Davinal Diggers superstar Greg Scott was best on ground, kicking nine goals in an easy preliminary final win over the Gregtown Goannas. Playing in the midfield,

Scott was his usual unstoppable self, thrilling the crowd with a number of spectacular marks.

As Fox was reading, Mr Scott walked into the changing rooms.

"Did you *ever* play a bad game?" Fox asked his coach.

Chase wandered over bouncing a footy and said, "Yeah, Mr Scott, you must have been the local hero."

But Mr Scott shook his head. "That guy is the only true hero I've ever met," he said, pointing to where Snowy Davison was standing.

Fox was about to ask his coach what he meant when Samantha Lu arrived and Mr Scott left the conversation to go and give her a big kiss.

"Oh, gross!" called out Chase.

Later that morning, Fox watched his brother lead the Diggers under-11s to a convincing win over the Drongos. Even though it was a one-sided game, Fox had to admit that Magnus and Murdoch Winter played brilliantly for the opposition. They were fast and skilful—but just like their older brother, they were very bad sports.

They yelled at the umpire, their Diggers opponents, and even their own teammates.

"Hey, at least they're consistent," said Lewis. "They abuse *everyone*!"

Fox was also very impressed with Hugo's coaching

ability. He had read all of the emails Cyril had sent about tactics and was able to explain them in a way that was easy for the under-11s players to understand. Hugo also made sure everyone had a decent amount of time on the field, and during the breaks the players hung on his every word. And his job was certainly a lot easier now he didn't have to do it in secret!

The team's "official" coach, Mr Percy, was so uninterested in the final he brought along a violin, which he practised with his back to the game. He certainly needed to practise, as even with his expensive-looking instrument he still managed to make a sound like a cat being sick.

After the under-11s had beaten the Drongos by 37 points, it was the under-14s turn to take on the Stingrays.

Mr Scott started Simon off on the bench and didn't bring him onto the ground until the second half, by which stage the Diggers were well in control. Simon eagerly ran out to take up his position in the forward line.

Sammy tapped the ball to Chung, who quickly handballed to Rosie, who skilfully dodged to her left then looped a handpass over to Fox, who was moving at top pace. He took a bounce, then spotted Simon leading out from the goalsquare and speared a low-trajectory pass right into the full-forward's outstretched hands.

The crowd cheered loudly, and then fell into a nervous silence as Simon went back to take his shot for goal. He took a deep breath and ran in, watching the ball closely as he guided it onto his boot. It flew straight over the goal umpire's hat.

"Great goal!" shouted Fox as car horns sounded around the ground.

Diggers players rushed in from everywhere to congratulate Simon, with Mo Officer even sprinting all the way from full-back to say, "Grscmbakma!"

Simon wasn't 100 per cent sure what Mo had said, but he knew from the smile on his face that it was a compliment.

A DIGGER DEPARTS

In the crowd, the Diggers' oldest supporter, Snowy Davison, turned to Matilda Wall and said, "Simon is the most reliable kick for goal since Greg Scott."

Simon managed to slot three more majors and the Diggers won comfortably by nine goals. This was despite some sensational performances by the Stingrays' stars, Rob 'The Birdman' Stewart, Strawbs O'Dwyer and Seb Westin, who all tried their hearts out. In the end, the Diggers just had too many good players all over the field. The last quarter was a particularly unlucky one for Stonewarren, as The Birdman, Strawbs and Seb were forced off the ground with injuries.

The win meant the Diggers went straight into the Grand Final in two weeks' time, while the Stingrays had another chance the following Saturday, when they would play the winner of the game between the third- and fourth-placed teams. This turned out to be the Drongos—but only just.

Mace's team had gotten very lucky in the elimination final, sneaking victory by three points thanks to the Roosters' extremely inaccurate kicking. The final scoreboard read:

| Davinal Drongos | 11.3 (69) |
| Romana Roosters | 8.18 (66) |

The Drongos were even luckier the next week, because the Stingrays' three best players were kept out of the match by the injuries they had received during the game against the Diggers.

Stonewarren battled bravely without The Birdman, Strawbs and Seb, but eventually lost to the Drongos by just two points in another thriller.

The Drongos under-11s also won their qualifying final, which meant both Diggers teams would play their crosstown rivals in the Grand Final.

Fox lay on his bed daydreaming. It was the Sunday afternoon after the preliminary final and the Grand Final was still six days away, but it was all he could think about. He never took anything for granted, but knew if the Diggers played as a team they would beat the Drongos—unless something catastrophic happened. Suddenly, his thoughts were interrupted by the sound of the phone.

"Is someone going to get that?" called out Fox. The silence that followed his question suggested the answer was no, so he leapt off his bed and ran to grab it.

"Hello, Fox Swift speaking."

"Oh, hi Fox, it's Matilda Wall."

Fox could tell by the sound of Matilda's wavering voice that something was wrong.

"It's Snowy Davison ... He ... he ... passed away last night."

20

Two Finals and a Funeral

Matilda started sobbing and Fox could feel a lump in his throat.

He wanted to say something comforting, but the only words he could manage were, "I'm so sorry."

Matilda quietly blew her nose and regained her composure.

"Fox, I wonder if you can do me a favour?"

"Of course, anything."

"Could you tell Mo? They were such great mates and Snowy loved working with him."

"Sure," said Fox gently as Matilda began to cry again. "And if there's anything else my family or I can do, please let us know."

Fox felt sick in the stomach when he hung up the phone. Snowy Davison had been one of the Diggers' greatest supporters. With his amazing carpentry skills, he and Mo had rebuilt the clubrooms, the grandstand and the boundary fence. They had even replaced the horrendously crooked goalposts. And when Mace had set up a nasty Facebook page that featured horrible comments about the Diggers players, it was Snowy who had spoken to the local newspaper and forced the site to be taken down.

Fox went out to the garage and grabbed his bike. Breaking the news to Mo was going to be the hardest thing he had ever done in his life, but he wanted to speak to his friend in person, rather than over the phone.

When he got to the farm, he rode up the long driveway and knocked on the front door of the house. As always, Mrs Officer greeted him with a warm smile, even though her family faced losing their farm. Fox told her why he was there and she directed him to the far paddock, where Mo was fixing a gate that had become unhinged. Fox borrowed one of the Officers' motorbikes and headed out to deliver the bad news.

When Mo saw his friend, he grinned and asked if he'd come to help him fix the gate. Well, that's what Fox assumed he had said—what it actually sounded like was, "Uhertafxdagut?"

"Mo, I'm really sorry, but I have some bad news," said Fox. "Snowy Davison died last night."

The grin left Mo's face and his eyes narrowed. "Thanxfaletinmeno," he said. "Hewuzarippablok."

After an awkward silence, Fox said, "Is there anything you'd like me to do?"

"Nasheezritemat. Bettafixdafenz."

"Okay," said Fox, and Mo went straight back to work.

Fox turned and walked slowly back to the motorbike. As he hopped on, he glanced back and noticed his friend was not really working, but leaning on the fence and staring off into the distance.

The next day the headline of the *Davinal Digest* read: "Local Hero Passes Away Aged 90".

The article included some amazing stories about Snowy's bravery. Fox had known and chatted to this man for three years, and Snowy had never once boasted about his heroic past. According to the article, during World War II Snowy had risked his life many times to save wounded mates on the battlefield, and had received a very special medal called the Victoria Cross.

Everyone in town had a story about Snowy helping them out in some way over the years, and Bazza and Shazza were flooded with callers wanting to share their memories and express their sadness. Even Miles rang in to say how much the old soldier would be missed.

Shazza: Hi, you're speaking to Shazza and Bazza.

Miles: Hello, it's Miles P. Winter the Second here—

Shazza: Miles? How come *you're* calling in?

Bazza: Yeah, you must have the wrong number—

Miles: No, no, I just wanted to say what a fantastic bloke Blondie was—

Shazza: Blondie? You mean Snowy?

Miles: Yes, Snow-ee. We were great mates—

Bazza: Great mates?! Didn't you try to have his driving licence taken away?

Miles: Oh, that was just a—

Bazza and Shazza: Misunderstanding!

Sound Effect: Heavenly choir

Shazza: And didn't he challenge you to a driving competition?

Miles: Well, um, ahh …

Bazza: And didn't he thrash you?

Miles: Well I don't know if "thrash" is the right word.

Shazza: To all our listeners, if you were there on the day that Snowy Davison thrashed Miles in the driving competition, please give us a call!

Bazza: The switchboard is lighting up! Looks like lots of people want to talk about it.

Miles: I really don't think there's any need to bring that up. I just wanted to say goodbye to my good friend Blondie—

Shazza: Snowy.

Miles: Snowy.

Bazza: By the way, how's your farting problem going, Miles?

Miles: I don't have a farting problem!

Sound Effect: Farting noise

Shazza: Ohhhhh Miles!

Miles: But that wasn't me!

Bazza: Then prove it by *not* farting.

Miles: Okay, I—

Sound Effect: Farting noise

Shazza: Guilty!

Miles: But, but, but—

Bazza: It's your *butt* that is the problem, Miles!

Shazza: Yeah, put a cork in it, Miles—literally. Let's take another call.

People travelled to Davinal from all over the world to pay their respects at Snowy's funeral. There were also several politicians and some television news reporters.

"I wonder if the politicians would turn up if there weren't any TV cameras?" said Mr Swift as he drove his family towards the church.

As they went past the local RSL, Fox noticed the flag was at half mast.

Hugo's dad was the local priest and he gave a moving service in honour of Snowy. Mo had done an exceptional job making Snowy's coffin, which stood in pride of place in front of the altar. It was draped in an Australian flag and also had a Diggers football jumper lying on top of it.

Mo also gave a speech. When he finished, all the females around Fox cried and said it was beautiful, but Fox and Lewis simply looked at each other and shrugged their shoulders—neither of them had understood a word. Mo then picked up his guitar and sang a song called *Hurt* that he'd seen his hero Johnny Cash singing on YouTube.

Fox heard Zebidiah Fontaine explain to Chase that the song was originally by a band called Nine Inch Nails, but that he preferred Johnny Cash's version. Chase nodded wisely, but Fox was pretty sure his

TWO FINALS AND A FUNERAL

brother did not have a clue who either Johnny Cash or the Nine Inch Nails were.

Unlike his speaking voice, Mo's singing voice was clear and strong, and when he sang the final words—"I will find a way"—*everyone* cried, stood up and applauded.

Lewis whispered to Fox, "If Mo went on that reality TV show *Farmer Wants A Wife*, he would win for sure!"

At the end of the service, Fox watched Mo and some of Snowy's older friends carry the coffin out of the church to the cemetery. He wasn't sure how Snowy's death would affect the Diggers in the Grand Final, but he made a promise to himself that he wouldn't let their former number one supporter down.

On Grand Final day, both the Diggers under-11s and under-14s agreed to wear black armbands as a mark of respect for Snowy.

The home crowd roared as Chase led his team through the inspirational banner.

Magnus and Murdoch Winter did not believe their team had a chance of defeating the Diggers, so they did what came naturally to them—they cheated! After sneaking a bottle of liquid laxative from their house, they poured it into the Diggers' cordial before the start of the game.

"That should give them an *explosive* start to the game," said Murdoch, high-fiving his brother.

Unfortunately for the twins, Lewis overheard them talking about their devious plan and discreetly switched the teams' drinks.

As a result, during the game the Drongos players were constantly running off the field for a visit to the toilet. This made the Diggers' job much easier, and with Chase and Jimmy picking up kicks all over the ground, the home team won by nearly 10 goals. When the siren sounded all the players rushed over to thank Hugo for all the help he had given them throughout the year.

Even though Mr Percy hadn't really coached the team, he still tried to take all the credit by wandering over to a large group of Diggers supporters and taking a bow. The crowd was staring back at him, not really sure what to do, when all of a sudden Joey came up from behind and kicked Mr Percy in the bum! There was a lot of applause and laughter as the Diggers mascot then chased the disgraced so-called coach out of the car park.

As thoughts now turned to the day's next match, the Diggers under-14s were given a huge boost when Cyril Rioli arrived just before the game and gave them a pep talk.

"You guys will win today if you're all prepared to work hard for each other—so are you?"

"Yes!"

"Are you going to tackle and chase all day, even when you're absolutely exhausted?"

"Yes!"

"Is every one of you going to give 100 per cent in every contest for four quarters?"

"Yes!"

By the time they ran out onto the ground Fox knew his team was going to play well. He had never seen his teammates so pumped up.

"LezdoifaSnow!" roared Mo Officer.

And they did. Simon started on the ground and kicked four first-half goals. Fox, Rosie and Chung starred in the middle, often receiving perfect hit-outs from Sammy and Chris. Paige was dynamic in the forward line and her two early goals were followed up by two spectacular backflips. In the backline, Mo and Bruno marked everything and Laser flashed by them repeatedly to take handballs and pump the ball deep into the forward line. At half-time Fox could not believe his eyes when he looked across at the scoreboard.

| Diggers | 12.4 (76) |
| Visitors | 3.2 (20) |

"I knew we were winning," he thought, "but by 56 points? Wow!"

Walking back to the changing rooms, Fox received another huge surprise when a large modern bus pulled into the car park and a group of kids in school uniform stepped off it, as well as some of the boys he had met from the Tiwi Islands.

"Good on you, Fox Swift!" yelled out Junior.

Fox gave Junior and his Tiwi Island mates a thumbs up before walking into the changing rooms.

"I have no idea why they're here," he whispered to Lewis, "but how cool is it to have the Tiwi boys in Davinal?"

In the second half, Fox and his team turned in a fantastic performance, and the Tiwi boys and their private school friends from Exford College were very impressed. Simon ended up kicking seven goals, Fox kicked six and Paige kicked five in one of the most one-sided Grand Finals seen on the Diggers' home ground.

| Diggers | 26.12 (168) |
| Visitors | 7.5 (47) |

However, there was no denying Vince had played a very good game for the Drongos, and Fox had heard the constant encouragement he had given his teammates. Mace, on the other hand, had repeatedly screamed at his players for making mistakes, before limping off in the last quarter with a fake ankle injury.

Fox thought it was strange how well Mr Winter was taking the loss. Normally he would be frothing at the mouth, but today he seemed more interested in reading the business section of the newspaper. He'd even kept his cool when the lol-ing kookaburra had flown over to the Diggers ground. Whenever the kookaburra had started laughing after a Diggers goal, Miles had just shrugged his shoulders and muttered something about the price of gold going up.

Cyril, who had been standing with the Tiwi boys in the second half, joined the Diggers circle next to Mr Scott as the players sang the club song—three times in a row!

Fox had never heard the Diggers sing the song so loudly.

Oh we're from Diggerland
A fighting fury, we're from Diggerland
In any weather you will see us with a grin
Risking head and skin
If we're behind, then never mind we'll fight and fight and win
For we're from Diggerland
We never weaken 'til the final siren's gone

Like the Diggers of old
We're strong and we're bold
Oh we're from Digger ...
YELLOW AND BLUE
For we're from Diggerland!

As usual, Lewis squirted everyone with water when they sang "YELLOW AND BLUE!" so they were all completely drenched by the time they finished the third rendition.

Both teams stayed on the ground after the game for the presentation ceremony. The junior league president, Mabel Hurley, gave the Drongos players their runners-up medallions and the Diggers ones inscribed with the word "premiers".

Shortly after all the players had received their medallions, a well-dressed, fit-looking man in a suit wandered over to where Fox and some of the players were standing.

"Hi!" he said to Fox in a friendly voice. "My name is Mr Tatty and I'm the principal of Exford College."

"Hi, I'm Fox Swift," replied the Diggers captain, shaking his hand.

"I know that," said the principal. "Congratulations on the win today! What I'd like to do is offer you a full scholarship to come to our school as a boarder next year."

Fox was speechless.

"You don't have to make a decision yet, and you'll need to talk it over with your parents, but if you decide to come you may already know a few of the students."

"Really?" said Fox.

"Yes, because I'm also offering scholarships to Paige Turner for gymnastics, and Lewis Rioli and Rosie McHusky for athletics—"

At this point Hugo and Chung came over and said hello to Mr Tatty.

Fox looked surprised.

"Hugo and Chung recently sat an exam for an academic scholarship to the school," explained Mr Tatty, "and they were both successful."

"We wanted to tell you, Fox, but we had to wait until it was official," said Hugo.

Mace, who had been listening in on the conversation with his father, went up to the principal and said, "Hey, I sat that exam! How come I didn't get a scholarship?"

"Well, um, we only give out academic scholarships to the very brightest students in the country—oh, hello Vince."

Mace's eyes widened. "How do you know Vince?" he asked.

"I sat that exam, too," Vince said sheepishly, "and I kind of won a science scholarship."

"Well it must be a school for stupid people," hissed Mace.

"Don't worry, son," said Miles. "Soon we're going to be able to afford to send you to any school you want, anywhere in the world."

The Tiwi College boys then came over to chat to Fox, and Mr Tatty explained they were on their annual visit to Exford College.

"The boys said they had met you and Lewis earlier this year," he said. "So I thought coming along today was a good chance for you to catch up, and for me to offer you, Lewis, Rosie and Paige the scholarships in person."

"Hey, if Fox goes to Exford College, can he play for Tiwi College in the annual footy match?" asked Junior. "Because he's an honorary Tiwi!"

Mr Tatty thought about this for a while and said, "It's okay with me, so as long as it's okay with Fox?"

A huge smile appeared on Fox's face.

"Definitely!" he said.

21

Bank You Very Much

The next morning Fox woke up in a great mood. As he headed down for breakfast, he had to keep pinching himself to make sure he wasn't still dreaming and the Diggers really had won three flags in a row.

He walked into the kitchen to find his mum and dad sitting at the table. They stopped talking as soon as he entered the room.

"What is it?" asked Fox. "Did Chase forget to flush the toilet again?"

"No," said Mrs Swift with a sad look on her face. "We've just had a call from Mrs Officer. They are going to have to sell their farm next Saturday."

"They've asked your mum and me to do all the legal paperwork," said Mr Swift.

"This is so not fair!" said Fox.

"You're right," sighed Mrs Swift. "But unfortunately the Officers owe the bank a lot of money, and unless they can repay it by 2pm on Saturday, they'll have no choice but to sell their farm to Selim Properties."

Fox frowned and decided to do what he always did when he didn't have an answer—ring Hugo.

"We have to do *something*!" said Fox to his incredibly smart friend. "I just don't have a clue what that something is!"

"Mmmm ... I'll see what I can do," said Hugo.

Hugo had been spending a lot of time at the Davinal historical centre over the past few months. The first time he'd told everyone he was going there Lewis had misheard him and said, "That sounds like fun!"

In the coming week Hugo would spend even more time—every spare second in fact—at the historical centre, reading dozens of dusty old books and making pages and pages of notes.

He was still there on the Saturday that the Officers' farm was to be sold, and was by now very anxious because he knew he was running out of time. He took off his glasses and took a few deep breaths as he rubbed his tired eyes. He had just put his glasses back on and was about to read through his notes again, when he suddenly spotted a small, battered-looking book poking out from the bookshelf. Almost without thinking, he left his chair and went to retrieve it. It looked like a handwritten diary.

Hugo flicked through the pages and was convinced he had discovered an important clue—there was only one problem: it was written in Chinese.

Picking up his smartphone, Hugo took photos of the relevant pages and sent them in a text to Chung's father, Feng, with the words, "Mr Lee, can you please translate this ASAP?"

Ten minutes later, his phone buzzed. Hugo read Mr Lee's response and smiled, then dialled Fox's number.

"Fox, I haven't got time to explain but we need to get a group of Diggers out to Mo's farm immediately, and also someone has to go to the bank and stall the sale, okay?"

"Done," said Fox. He had no idea what Hugo's plan was, but he trusted him completely.

He quickly organised for Lewis, Paige, Bruno, Rosie, Simon and Aslam to meet him at the farm. As for finding a person to delay the signing of the contract, Fox knew straight away who to call.

The phone was picked up after a couple of rings.

"Chung, I have a job for you ..."

When Fox arrived at the farm, Hugo was already there chatting to Mo. Mr and Mrs Officer had left half an hour earlier to meet with Fox's parents before going to the bank.

The other Diggers Fox had phoned arrived a few minutes later and Hugo immediately gave them instructions.

"Okay, everyone into the back of the ute. Mo, take us to the paddock where we helped put out the fire."

Everyone did as they were told, and in no time they had reached the paddock.

Hugo, who was sitting in the front of the ute next to Mo, pointed to a tree and said, "Over there, that's where we need to go."

Mo turned the wheel and sped over to a giant old gum tree. They all jumped out and waited for further instructions.

Hugo took charge. "I want you all to start at the tree and then fan out in different directions. Keep looking down, and if you see a patch of soil that looks different from the ground around it, yell out. Got it?"

"Got it!" said his friends as they began their search.

All of a sudden Lewis called out, "Hey, I think the soil is dif—Aghhhhhhhhh!"

There was a crashing sound as the earth beneath Lewis gave way and he disappeared out of sight.

Fox rushed over and peered through the dust. There was a giant hole in the ground where Lewis used to be.

"Lewis, are you okay?!"

"Yes—although I would have been better if I hadn't landed on this giant rock! Ouch."

"Don't worry, we'll get you out of there. Can you see anything or is it pretty dark down there?"

"It's not too bad actually. This rock I landed on kind of glows a bit so—"

"Did you say it glows?" asked Hugo, barely able to contain his excitement. "Let's get it up here now!"

"Do you mean me or the stupid rock?" snapped Lewis.

"No offence, Lewis, but I mean the stupid rock," said Hugo. "Mo, do you have a winch we can use?"

Meanwhile, at the local bank in town, Mr Shloogal had a surprise visitor.

"Yes, how can I help you, young fella?" he asked as Chung entered his office.

"Mr Shloogal, my name is Chung and I'm interested in becoming a bank manager. Would it be okay if I hung out with you so I can learn about what you do?"

"Well, I'm pretty busy at the moment—"

"It's just that you're ... kind of my hero."

"Your hero? Really? Well, I suppose I could find something for you to do. The floor does need a bit of a sweep—there's a broom in the closet over there."

When Mr Shloogal wasn't looking, Chung rolled his eyes. He couldn't work out what was worse—having to sweep the floor or having to pretend that Mr Shloogal was his hero.

A short time later, Mr and Mrs Officer arrived with their legal representatives, Mr and Mrs Swift. They were all a bit surprised to see Chung sweeping in the corner.

"I'm his hero," said Mr Shloogal simply.

The Officers and Swifts exchanged looks and Chung blushed.

"I will never live this down," he thought to himself.

"Well," said Mr Shloogal, "we said we'd sign the contract at 2pm so let's—"

Mr Shloogal stopped speaking and stared at the clock on the wall. "That clock says it's only 1.30pm, it must have stopped—"

He checked his watch, which also said 1.30pm.

The Officers and Swifts checked their watches, and all confirmed that the time was indeed half past one.

As this was going on, Chung continued to sweep innocently in the background.

"Well that is strange," said Mr Shloogal, "but since you're here you may as well sign now."

"Ifitzkayiruthawaitato," said Mr Officer.

"Um, sorry?" said Mr Shloogal. "I didn't quite catch that."

"He said if it's okay he would prefer to delay the signing of the contract until the pre-arranged time of 2pm," said Mrs Officer.

Mrs Swift understood that Mr Officer hated the thought of selling the farm and didn't want it to happen any earlier than it had to.

"Let's go grab a coffee next door at Main Street Café and come back in half an hour then," she said.

"But, but—"

"No buts, Mr Shloogal," said Mr Swift, placing the folder he was carrying on the bank manager's desk. "We'll leave the contract here and be back at 2pm."

"Yes!" said Chung as they left.

"Why are you so happy?" Mr Shloogal asked suspiciously.

"Because, um … because it gives me a chance to ask you how you became a banker," said Chung.

"That's a funny story," said Mr Shloogal, "and it will probably take me at least half an hour—"

"Oh my God!" thought Chung. "Hugo better come up with something soon or I will die of boredom!"

Mo had gone and picked up the winch and was now lowering the rope to Lewis.

"TythruprownthrokLew!" he shouted.

There was silence from the hole until Paige yelled

BANK YOU VERY MUCH

down, "Tie the rope around the rock, Lewis!"

"Ohhhh," said Lewis.

He secured the rope to the rock as best he could, but this was a fairly difficult task because the rock was so heavy.

"Okay, bring her up," he called out a few minutes later.

Mo started winding the winch that was set up in the back of the ute, but even he wasn't strong enough to move the rock on his own, so Simon and Bruno jumped up to help. Slowly it began to inch upwards.

Fox and Aslam swapped places with Simon and Bruno to give them a break, and after 20 minutes of very hard work the enormous rock was finally above the ground.

They all stared. The huge rock was shaped like a giant footy boot. A giant *golden* footy boot.

"Is that what I think it is?" said Fox.

"It sure is," said Hugo. "Let's get it onto the back of the ute and then it's straight to the bank."

"Make sure you give my regards to Mr Shloogal!" called out an extremely sarcastic voice from the hole.

"Oh yeah, sorry about that, Lewis!" said Hugo sheepishly. "We'll winch you out in a minute."

"Okay, so let's sign the contract," said Mr Shloogal eagerly when the Officers and Swifts returned.

But when Mr Swift opened the folder it was empty.

"Where's the contract gone, Mr Shloogal?"

"I don't know!" said the bank manager. "I never touched it—I've been talking to Chung the whole time you were gone."

Mr Shloogal turned to Chung for support.

"He's right," said Chung. "Mr Shloogal was telling me a fascinating story about how he ended up in banking—hey, Mr Shloogal, why don't you tell these guys all about it? I swear it's an absolute crack-up—"

"We don't have time for that!" said the banker. "I'll just go print off another copy."

"Shoot," thought Chung.

Five minutes later, Mr Shloogal re-entered his office with a freshly printed copy of the contract in his hand. He plopped it front of the Officers, turned to the last page and said, "So if you could just sign here—"

"Hold on!" said Mrs Swift. "How do we know this contract is the same one as the last one?"

"Just take my word for it! So, Mr Officer, here's a pen—"

"No one is signing anything until we've re-read every word," Mrs Swift said firmly.

Mr Shloogal wanted to scream. Sweat appeared on his forehead, and he took a deep breath.

"Okay, okay! But can you read it *quickly*?"

After they had safely loaded the giant golden boot into the back of the ute, Mo covered it with a tarpaulin.

"How are we going to get to town, Mo?" asked Fox. "You're not allowed to drive on the roads."

"Idrythrunayborsfamstilwgittobedesunhiltoeusinaton."

"That's brilliant, Mo!" said Rosie as she and Paige high-fived him.

Fox had absolutely no idea what Mo had said but there was no time to find out, so, like everyone else, he jumped into the ute.

As Mo started driving through the paddocks, Rosie and Paige explained the plan.

"Mo reckons he can drive through other farms nearly all the way to town—all we have to is open and shut the gates," said Rosie

"And the last farm is owned by some friend of the Officers called 'Beardy', who has a tow truck business," said Paige. "Mo says he should be able to take the ute into town on the back of his truck."

Thanks to Mo's knowledge of all the shortcuts through neighbouring properties, they arrived at

Beardy's farm in less than 15 minutes. Standing out the front of a brown brick home was a man wearing a white grease-stained singlet, blue shorts and thongs. He had a gigantic black beard that stretched all the way past his rather large stomach.

"I'm guessing that's Beardy," said Lewis with a grin.

Beardy walked over to the ute and leaned up against the door.

"G'day Mo, how ya goin'?"

"Cnyatowmauteinatonitzamerginsy?"

Beardy didn't ask any questions. He just shrugged his shoulders and said, "No worries."

As Mo drove the ute up a ramp onto the back of Beardy's giant tow truck, Hugo looked at his watch.

"It's after 3pm," he said to Fox. "We may already be too late!"

"Have some faith in Chung," said Fox. "If anyone can slow down the signing, he can."

"That's true," said Hugo. "And if nothing holds us up, we're only about 10 minutes away."

Beardy's tow truck had such a large cabin that all the Diggers could fit inside comfortably. There was no traffic and they made it to the bank even faster than Hugo had calculated.

But as soon as they arrived, Beardy jumped out of the truck and announced, "Excuse me kids, but I'm busting to go to the toilet!"

And with that he dashed into Main Street Café.

"But Beardy, we need to get the ute off the truck *now*!" Fox called out after him.

"Donwuri," said Mo. "Ilgitiorf."

"No, you can't, Mo—you're not allowed to drive on the road," said Paige.

Fox realised Paige was technically correct. By driving the car off the truck and into the spare parking space Mo would be breaking the law. Even if it was only for 15 seconds.

"Ihaftawedonhavtime."

Hugo reached into his pocket and pulled out his stick-on detective's moustache. "Here, put this on, Mo. That way, if anyone sees you, hopefully they'll think you're your dad."

Mo put on the moustache, and climbed up onto the back of the truck. He jumped into the ute, started the engine and carefully began backing it down the ramp onto the street.

"Uh, oh!" said Fox looking at the road ahead.

A police car was coming towards them on the other side of the road, and behind the wheel was Sergeant Hunt.

As the police car passed by, Mo gave Sergeant Hunt a small wave with his finger like his dad always did.

Sergeant Hunt waved back and kept driving.

"All right!" said Fox, giving Hugo a high five.

He then turned to Mo and said, "Well don—um, your moustache has slipped."

Mo looked in the rear-view mirror and noticed that the police car had slowed down and pulled over to the side of the road.

"Wemibbusta," he said.

Sergeant Hunt had pulled over because he had suddenly realised there had been something very strange about Mr Officer. "What was it?" he thought to himself. "I know, his moustache!"

Back in Mr Shloogal's office, Mrs Swift had finished re-reading the contract.

"It all seems to be in order," she said with a sigh.

"Excellent! Now if the Officers could just sign it at the back. Here, use my pen—" said Mr Shloogal, patting his top pocket. "My pen! Where is my pen?"

He frantically stuck his hands in all of his pockets, but they were all empty.

"Has anyone got a pen?" he asked hopefully.

The Swifts and the Officers patted their pockets, but their pens had all mysteriously disappeared, too.

Chung sat quietly in the corner twiddling his thumbs.

"Don't worry," said Mr Shloogal. "I have a pen in the next room—excuse me for a second."

Mr Shloogal disappeared through a door near the back of his office, just as Mo was pulling back the tarpaulin on the ute.

The giant boot-shaped nugget was so heavy it took all nine of them to lift it off the back of the ute and carry it inside.

They burst in to Mr Shloogal's office just as Mr Officer was putting pen to paper.

"Dunsunitda!" yelled Mo.

"What?" said Mr Shloogal.

"He said, 'Don't sign the contract, Dad!'" said Rosie.

The Diggers heaved the giant golden nugget onto the desk, and a stunned Mr Shloogal could only look on as his desk collapsed under the enormous weight.

22

Case Closed

Everyone stared in silence at the massive gold nugget sitting on the flattened table.

"Lukwhutwefondondfum!" announced Mo with a grin.

Mr Officer looked at Mo, then looked back at the nugget.

"Yoozecngoanstikyaflamincntratupyabluddyjumpr!" he said to Mr Shloogal as he ripped the contract into tiny pieces.

"What did he say?" whispered Fox.

"It's a bit too rude to repeat," said Paige with a smile.

"We'll buy you a new table, Mr Shloogal," said Mrs Officer apologetically.

Mrs Swift gave Fox a hug. "How did you find it?" she asked.

"I think I'll hand over to Hugo to explain," said

Fox. "He was the genius who worked everything out."

Hugo put his hands behind his back and started pacing back and forth across the room.

"I suggest you all take a seat—this might take a while."

At that moment, the door flew open and in burst Sergeant Hunt. When he saw the gigantic gold nugget shaped like a footy boot, his mouth dropped open in shock.

"Sergeant Hunt, I suggest you take a seat as well, as I'm sure you will find this most interesting."

Sergeant Hunt wasn't used to taking orders from a 13-year-old boy, but he was so stunned by everything that was going on he sat straight down.

Hugo recommenced his pacing.

"As you may recall, a number of the Officers' sheep escaped onto the road earlier this year," he said.

Everyone in the room nodded.

"At the time, I thought it was strange that there were *quad bike* tyre tracks in paddock. You see, the Officers don't own a quad bike. So I put that clue together with the fact that Fox thought he had heard a motorbike the night before, and deduced that someone else had been in that paddock."

Fox smiled. He had no idea where his friend was going with his story, but he couldn't wait to find out.

"I inspected the fallen fence and it looked like the

wire had been sliced through with wire cutters."

Hugo went quiet to let this point sink in.

"Sabotage!" he yelled suddenly, making everyone jump.

"I then checked the fallen fence post and noted there were groove marks. This suggested that the fence had been pulled down by a rope attached to the quad bike."

Again Hugo paused for effect.

"Sabotage!" he yelled again.

This caused an outburst of excited chattering in the room, and Hugo held up his hand to quieten everyone so he could continue his story.

"Then there was the fire on the Officers' farm that occurred straight after an anonymous phone call about sheep being caught in a fence on the opposite side of the farm."

Fox remembered this well. He would never forget how hard they had worked to put out the fire.

"I also overheard the fire chief, Mr Mackay, saying he had been called out to another fire that turned out to be a false alarm, and that's why he and his firemen were late to get to the Officers' farm. That made me even more suspicious, so I *sniffed* around—and smelled petrol. It was strongest right near the patch where the fire had started. Yes, that fire was deliberately lit."

"Sabotage!" yelled out Lewis.

Hugo shot his friend a look that clearly said, "Hey, that's my line!"

"Sorry!" said Lewis sheepishly.

"Now, where was I? Oh, that's right—sabotage!" he cried, making everyone jump again.

"So who is responsible?" he asked. "Let's look at the following clues," he said before anyone could answer.

"I heard Mace Winter bragging that his father had bought a new quad bike at the end of last year."

Everyone was silent as Hugo began to spell out the case he had built against Miles Winter. Sergeant Hunt even pulled out a pen and started taking notes. He also wrote down the word "motive" followed by a big question mark.

"Sergeant Hunt, you're probably wondering what motive Mr Winter could have," said Hugo without even looking at the policeman.

"This kid is amazing!" thought Sergeant Hunt. "A little annoying, but quite amazing."

"The answer is money!" said Hugo suddenly. "Or, more specifically: *gold*."

This last word hung in the air, and everyone turned to look at the giant nugget.

"As most of you know, Davinal was a goldmining town way back in 1880s. We all also know that

Mr Winter suddenly started spending a lot of time at the historical centre this year, and the librarian, Mrs Savage, told me that the only books he ever took off the shelves were ones that mentioned 'Toothy' Taylor, the old prospector."

"What are you saying, Hugo?" said Sergeant Hunt.

"I'm saying that Mr Winter has been desperately searching for old Toothy's goldmine for well over a year. His plan was to buy up all the farmers' land at dirt-cheap prices. Some of the farmers were happy to leave the district because of the drought, but if they weren't … Well, Mr Winter would sneak onto to their farms and—"

Hugo stopped and nodded at Lewis, who yelled, "Sabotage!"

Hugo once again began pacing with his hands behind his back.

"Didn't anyone else think it was suspicious when Mr Winter started spending his weekends cleaning up the side of the highway near the farms with his metal detector? Was he really picking up cans to help the community … or was he trying to find the location of Toothy's gold?"

Fox had to agree with his friend—it was hard to imagine Mr Winter ever doing something from the goodness in his heart.

"But one of the biggest clues was when Fox saw

Mr Winter handing a leaf to a scientist when we visited the Synchrotron," said Hugo. "Thanks to the amazing technology at the Synchrotron, scientists can analyse a leaf and determine if a gold deposit lies under the tree it came from."

Chung nodded in agreement as Hugo continued.

"Mr Winter thought he could use modern technology like metal detectors and scientific reports from the Synchrotron to do what the miners of the 1880s and 1890s couldn't: find Toothy Taylor's gold!"

"Mmm, that's a good theory," said Sergeant Hunt, "but why do you think Mr Winter is the one who has been buying up all the farms in the area?"

"Good question!" said Hugo. "Sergeant Hunt, what is the name of the company that has been buying up all the land in the district?"

"Selim Properties."

"And what is Selim spelled backwards?"

Sergeant Hunt wrote it out on his pad: M-I-L-E-S.

"Miles!"

Everyone gasped in amazement. None of them had thought of this before.

"That son of a—"

"No wonder he was always going on about the price of gold!" said Fox.

"How were you able to find the gold before Mr Winter, Hugo?" asked Chung.

"I have your dad to thank for that," said Hugo.

Chung stared back at him blankly.

"This morning at the historical centre I discovered the diary of a Chinese miner called Tai Heng who had been a good friend of Toothy's. It was written in Chinese of course, so I took some pictures of the pages and sent them to Mr Lee to translate."

Chung beamed with pride.

"According to the date of the last entry in Tai Heng's diary, he left the district the day before Toothy struck it rich. He had gone over to say goodbye to Toothy at his digging site, and when he got there he swore he heard two people talking—but the only ones there were Toothy and his horse. Anyway, from Tai Heng's description of the gum tree where he said goodbye to his friend, I was able to pinpoint exactly where Toothy's final digging spot was."

Everyone burst into applause in appreciation of Hugo's brilliance.

"But don't forget that *I* was the genius who managed to fall into it," said Lewis, causing everyone to crack up with laughter.

"So is that the end of your detective work for the day?" asked Sergeant Hunt.

"Mmm, just one more thing—" said Hugo, walking over to the door near the back of Mr Shloogal's office. "I believe there is someone behind this door listening in to every word I'm saying—isn't there, Mr Winter?"

With that, Hugo flung open the door and Miles Winter fell into the room.

There was silence as Mr Winter jumped to his feet and dusted himself off.

"Hi," he said, trying to act as if everything was normal. "I was just, um, looking for ... my hat! I think I left it here after a meeting with Mr Shloogal last week. Anyone seen it? No? I best be going then."

Mr Winter started heading for the other door when he heard Sergeant Hunt clear his throat.

"Ahem! Not so fast, Mr Winter."

Hugo Holmes

Miles was very lucky that, because no one had actually seen him sabotaging the farms, Sergeant Hunt couldn't prove he had committed any crimes.

For this reason he managed to avoid going to jail—but only just. He was very unlucky, however, in that none of the farms he had purchased as Selim Properties turned out to have any gold on them at all—it was all on the Officers' farm.

The Golden Boot turned out to be worth a whopping $5 million, and so with all the other gold deposits found on their farm the Officers suddenly had more money than they knew what to do with. The *Davinal Digest* covered the story, running the headline, "Mo Worries!" next to a photo of the Officers all dressed up. Fox had never seen anyone look as uncomfortable in a suit as Mo—except maybe Mo's father! The accompanying article declared that at 78 kilograms, The Golden Boot would replace The Welcome Stranger as the biggest nugget ever discovered. None of the Diggers had heard of The Welcome Stranger—except of course for Hugo.

"It was discovered by John Deason and Richard Oates at Moliagul, Victoria on 5 February 1869," he helpfully informed them. "It was too big for the scales, so they had to break into three pieces to be able to weigh it!"

"A bit like your brain, Hugo!" joked Lewis.

Sergeant Hunt gave Mo a stern talking to for underage driving, and suspended him from driving on the road for three years. This sounded pretty harsh, but as Hugo pointed out, no one was allowed to go for their 'L' plates until they were 16 anyway.

Fox couldn't believe how quickly the year had raced by. And what a year it had been! There was the visit to the Tiwi Islands, the Nuggets' victory over the State Metro team, the Diggers' premiership, Hugo saving Mo's farm, and the offer of a scholarship to attend Exford College in the city next year.

Fox had made a decision with his parents that he would accept the scholarship. The decision was made much easier by the fact that Lewis, Hugo, Paige, Rosie and Chung would also be going there—as would Vince!

He knew that as a boarder he would miss his family, Mr Scott, Joey, Gary and all the Diggers, but he would be able to come home and visit a couple of times each term. And he was sure Chase would keep him up to date on everything via email—including a detailed account of how his amazing team was going.

On the last day of the school year, Mr Renton asked Fox to come in early and see him in his office.

The principal was filling out another survey for the Department of Education, which awarded an extra 10 points for an interview with the school captain at the end of term. But when Fox got there, the entire administration building was just a pile of rubble. All he could say was, "Wow!"

He had completely forgotten about Miss Carey and the termites.

Mr Renton was standing in front of the ruins with his hands on his head and a shocked look on his face. Miss Carey was beside him looking triumphant.

"I got it! I got it!" she cried, holding up a microscopic creature with a pair of tweezers.

"What do you mean *it*? Don't you mean *them*?" said Mr Renton.

"No, it turns out there was just one of them," said Miss Carey, dropping the tiny insect into a test tube.

"What?!" screamed Mr Renton

Fox shrugged his shoulders and said, "In Miss Carey's defence, she did say that *one* termite could bring down an entire building."

Mr Renton looked like he was about to explode, so Fox quickly slipped away.

On the way to class, Fox spotted Vince talking and laughing with Chung and Hugo ahead of him. When they got to the classroom, Chung and Hugo went to put their books in their lockers and Mace came over to speak Vince.

"Hey Vince, you want to throw some rocks at the train after school?"

"Um, I kinda said I'd help Hugo and Chung with something. We're going to do that Bragg Defraction Experiment—"

Mace was furious and went bright red.

"Vince, you need to decide—you are either with those losers or you're with me!"

Vince thought very carefully about what Mace had just said before calling out, "Hugo, Chung! Wait up!"

"You're making a big mistake, Vince!" shouted Mace.

Vince stopped, turned around and walked back. Looking his former friend directly in the eye, he said, "Shut up, Mace."

A Quirky Footy Dictionary

Acute angle—the word acute means severe. For example, there's acute pain, acute boredom, a cute puppy—wait, that's something different. If you are on an acute angle, it means you are kicking at goal from right on the boundary line. It's a very difficult kick, but if you do manage to slot it, the really hard part is pretending it wasn't a fluke. You have to give a look that says, "What? I kick these all the time." This will give your opponent an acute headache.

Brownlow Medal—normally things that are brown and low are flushed down the toilet, but a Brownlow Medal (named after the former Geelong administrator and player Charles 'Chas' Brownlow) is the highest individual honour in the AFL. After each game, the umpires secretly award votes to the three players they think were the fairest and best on the ground. Nobody knows how many votes any player has received until they are read out at a ceremony at the end of the season. The player with the most votes wins the medal, so it always pays to be nice to the umpires!

Caught holding the ball—this is where the police burst onto the field and yell, "Freeze!" because they've caught you playing with a stolen football. It's also where you're tackled by an opposition player and you fail to get rid of the ball, resulting in a free kick being awarded against you.

Closing down space—if your opponents are really slack, you seem to have forever to pick up the ball and decide what to do with it. You have so much time and space you could make a cup of tea or get a pizza delivered before giving off a handball. But good teams close down your time and space by tackling you as soon as you grab the footy. You barely have time to get boot to ball, let alone dial the pizza delivery place.

Creative handballs—Australian artist Sidney Nolan used to dunk a footy in paint then handball it at the canvas. It is a little known fact that this is how his legendary Ned Kelly paintings were done. Skilful footballers are said to perform a creative handball when they handball to a teammate who is suddenly in the clear.

Burpee—this word sounds like the name for a tiny little burp, but it is really a very tiring exercise. You start off standing before dropping into a low squat with your hands on the ground and kicking your feet back, keeping your arms extended like you're about to do a push-up. Then you spring back to the low squat, jump up in the air and start all over again! Try it and see how many you can do without collapsing. I normally give up after three.

Drongos—way back in the 1920s there was a racehorse called Drongo who ran 37 times without ever winning. As a result, 'Drongo' became Australian slang for a no-hoper—think 'doofus' or 'dunderhead'. It is not a good nickname for a person … or a team.

Falcon—this is where a player is accidentally hit in the head with a footy. Personally, I think this is very unfair to falcons, which are a very coordinated type of bird. It also raises the question, if falcons get hit on the head by a footy, do they say, "I've been human-ed"?

Gathered possession—is just a very fancy way to say grabbing the ball. It's like saying, "I am transporting myself to the bathroom!" instead of, "I'm going to the dunny!"

Give and go—sometimes pushy charity collectors wander onto football ovals during games. The 'Give and Go' is where they stop a half-forward flanker and don't let them pass until they've made a donation. It is also where a player does a quick handball to a teammate, and then immediately calls for the ball back. It's a smart play because it doubles a player's stats.

Goal sneaks—these are the players who seem to kick goals when no one is looking. At the end of the game you think they only kicked one or two, but then you read in the newspaper the next day that they kicked five. This leads to a suspicion they must have kicked those extra goals during the quarter-time break, but in truth a good goal sneak simply makes the most of their chances and doesn't draw a lot of attention to themselves.

Having a picnic—if you are playing against a really friendly team their runner will sometimes bring out a tartan rug and a picnic basket and offer you a chicken sandwich and slice of cake at half-time. To be honest, this is pretty rare, and 'having a picnic' normally refers to when a team is having a lot of fun because they are picking up lots of easy kicks under no pressure.

Kicking a bag—in the olden days, if players were upset the runner would hand them an old brown sack and they would let out their frustrations by kicking it. However, in 1968, the Cruelty to Bags movement complained and this behaviour was outlawed. Kicking a bag nowadays means that one player has kicked so many goals you would need a bag to fit them in.

Kicked truly—a dishonest kick is one that lies all the time. It says things like, "I *promise* I'll go straight through the goals," and then it disappears over the boundary line instead—and then you realise it's stolen your wallet. Kicking truly means kicking straight, so the ball goes directly through the goals. (And doesn't steal your money.)

Large Hadron Collider—this sounds like a tough, slightly overweight player for the Hadron Football Club who likes smashing into opponents, but it is really a gigantic circular machine in Europe that smashes tiny sub-atomic particles together. The scientists in charge claim this helps them understand the universe, but they really do it because they think smashing things together is fun. Basically, scientists are just big kids, but they think no one will notice because they're wearing white lab coats and using big words like photosynthesis.

On the burst—it's important not to drink too much cordial before the game or when you bend down to pick up the ball it will feel like your bladder is about to explode. This is one definition of 'playing on the burst'. The other way to play on the burst is to receive a handball from a teammate when you are travelling at top speed, and you 'burst' past your opponents.

One-percenters—things like shepherding, chasing and smothering are referred to as the 'one-percenters', and you always hear coaches telling their players, "Just concentrate on the one-percenters and we'll win!" Mmmm, I'm no maths teacher, but if you ignore the other 99 per cent you *might* be in trouble.

Paddle the ball—on really wet days, footballers often take to the field in kayaks and use their paddles to move the ball towards goal. On dry days, when a player taps the ball in front of them a few times to make it easier to pick up, it is also called 'paddling the ball'.

Point-blank range—if another kid shoots you with a water pistol from point-blank range, it means they are very, very close to you—and you will be absolutely soaked. If you miss a goal when you are *kicking* from point-blank range, there is a good chance your coach will want to *shoot* you with a water pistol.

Ruck-rover—this is a very confused player who is not sure if they are a ruckman or a rover. It would be exactly the same if you were a bullfrog—you'd be asking yourself, "Am I a bull or am I frog?" I'd love to see a bullfrog talking to a sheepdog—now that would be a confusing conversation! Anyway, ruck-rovers tend to be too tall to be a rover, but not tall enough to be a ruckman, so they sometimes end up playing both roles.

Run off him—if you find yourself standing on a male opponent's head you should *run* off him immediately—not slowly jog off, or moonwalk off, but *run* off because they would be in a lot of pain. If your opponent is lazy or just really puffed out, you can take advantage of this by running off them down the field to call for the ball. You will be amazed at how many easy kicks you pick up.

Selling candy—because a lot of players run out of energy during a game, smart footballers worked out they could make some money by selling lollies on the field, but coaches didn't like this so they had to do it secretly—"Psst, wanna buy a snake?" "Shhh, sherbert?" Selling candy is also where players hold out the ball and the opposition player lunges for it (like it's candy) and the player sidesteps or baulks around them.

Spoiled each other—don't you hate those people who spoil films by telling everyone the ending? They'll just casually drop into conversation, "Wasn't it cool in Harry Potter when Snape turned out to be a good guy? Oh, you haven't seen *The Deathly Hallows: Part 2*? Sorry!" There is nothing worse!* Well, spoiling each other on the footy field is almost as bad, as it's when two teammates compete for the ball and ruin each other's chances of gaining possession. *If you haven't seen Harry Potter and the Deathly Hallows: Part 2, um ... sorry.*

Stoppages—this doesn't mean the game *stops* for *ages*—in fact it only stops for a very short time before it is re-started by a ball-up or a throw-in.

Time trial—if the siren goes off early there is usually a court case to determine if the timekeeper should go to prison and this is referred to as a time trial. Another version of a time trial is during pre-season training when the players have to run a set distance and the coach times them to see how fit they are.

Torpedo punt—a torpedo can sink a ship, and a torpedo punt can sink the opposition. The ball is kicked fairly flat off the boot so that it spirals through the air like a torpedo and travels a long way. While you get more distance with a 'torp', it is a difficult kick to master, and if a ball accidentally flies off the side of a player's boot the coach tends to become quite upset.

Turned the ball over—if you run out of food and all you have left to eat is a football, it is obviously important that you cook it properly. You don't want one side to be burnt and the other side to be raw, do you? For that reason it is important that you turn it over. On the field, if one side fumbles or miskicks the ball and it is picked up by the opposition the ball is said to have been turned over.

White line fever—when some players run onto the field and step over the white boundary line, they are instantly transformed—suddenly their smiles disappear, their eyes glaze over and they froth starts appearing in their mouth, like they have been possessed by a demon. These players are said to have been struck by white line fever. After the siren goes, having pulverised you all game, they are then happy to have a friendly chat and offer you a lift to the hospital.

Worm burner—this is a pass that is so low and fast it threatens to burst into flames and burn any unsuspecting worms in its path.

AUTHOR'S NOTE
BY DAVID LAWRENCE

1. Tiwi Islands

It was fantastic to brainstorm ideas about Fox's Tiwi Island visit with the local school children. Fortunately, the Tiwi Islands are a beautiful place to visit and much safer than Fox and his mates made it seem! After reading the first draft, the Tiwi kids told me that, unlike Fox's story, they would never risk putting Fox and Chase in danger by taking him swimming anywhere near crocodiles or jellyfish! Instead, they would have taken their visitors to a freshwater waterhole, where there was no way Chase could have been stung by jellyfish. (Although they pointed out he could have bitten by a water monitor, or a long neck turtle or a freshwater lobster!!) This story is fiction and meant to entertain, but I want to stress that we should never take lightly the dangers of some of our more prickly, bitey or stingy Australian wildlife. Fox and his friends were very lucky not to have been seriously hurt (even in the fictional account), so be very careful when you're out in the bush or going for a swim, and always check with an adult and let them know exactly where you're going. With that in mind, here are a few fun facts about jellyfish and crocodiles:

Crocodile—you know that saying 'Never smile at a

crocodile'? Well, it's no joke. The male saltwater crocodile can grow up to 6.7 metres and weigh up to a whopping 2000 kilograms, and has an even worse temper than Miles Winter. They will eat just about anything that wanders into their territory—even other crocodiles! They might look like big lazy logs floating in the water, but in short bursts crocodiles can swim three times faster than the fastest human swimmers, and even on land they can reach speeds of up to 18 kilometres an hour over short distances. In other words, you don't want one chasing you, so never smile, grin, laugh at or tease a crocodile.

Jellyfish—of all the things that sound harmless but are actually dangerous, jellyfish have to be right up near the top of the list. I mean, how scary is jelly? Scary delicious maybe. They sound like something you'd find in the lolly isle between the jelly babies and sugary snakes,

AUTHOR'S NOTE

but really jellyfish are found in the ocean all around Australia, and particularly in the tropics. In the Tiwi Islands, they are (much more sensibly) referred to as "stingers", and sting they do, as Chase found out in our story. The sting of a jellyfish can be extremely painful and sometimes even deadly. So if you're ever headed to the beach for a swim and you see even grown adults running out of the water and screaming like the Bogey man is after them, there is a good chance it's stinger season—and maybe you should consider going to the pool instead. If there are likely to be dangerous stingers in the water, there will sure to be signs around, warning swimmers to take care; and, in some cases, to not swim at all in the near regions.

2. The Synchrotron

I am embarrassed to say I didn't know Australia had a Synchrotron. (It's in south-east Melbourne.) Obviously I'm even more embarrassed to say that I didn't actually know what a Synchrotron was. (In case you're not too sure either, check out this excellent and informative website: *http://www.synchrotron.org.au*)

Through a bizarre series of events I ended up being given a tour of this massive structure, which is about the size of the MCG, late last year. I was completely blown away by the projects and experiments being conducted, which were all related to improving our lives.

I am your classic sports-loving, humanities type of guy, whose scientific knowledge is on par with Mr Grinter's, but to hear the passion of some of the scientists at the Synchrotron was truly inspiring. It was important to give some exposure to the Synchrotron in *Fox Swift and the Golden Boot* to encourage as many schools as possible to visit this incredible place. Hopefully these visits will inspire a number of students to become scientists who will one day discover cures to all types of diseases and illnesses—especially any I might contract!

ACKNOWLEDGEMENTS

If someone had told me in 2013 that there were going to be three *Fox Swift* books, I would have said, "Only three?" But then again, I am a ridiculously optimistic person.

Fox Swift has become a popular series because of the hard work, talent and support of a lot of people.

To the publisher, Geoff Slattery, thanks for really getting behind *Fox Swift and the Golden Boot*. Hopefully we have created a series that will put a smile on a lot of faces over a number of years.

A huge thank you to Jo Gill, whose wonderful drawings make the stories and the character of Lewis Rioli come alive. Readers love the cartoons, which add an extra layer of entertainment and make the books more accessible. Jo can act, write, draw and sing, which in showbiz circles makes her a quadruple threat.

It has been fantastic to once again team up with Cyril Rioli. The hard work he put in to his rehabilitation in 2014 in order to make it back for the Grand Final was nothing short of remarkable, and directly inspired one of the storylines in *Fox Swift and the Golden Boot*. So thanks again, Cyril, and fingers crossed for the three-peat. (Unless you end up playing the Bombers in the Grand Final, then may the best team win ... as long as it's Essendon.)

Speaking of three-peats, thanks to the amazing Bronwyn Wilkie for editing her third consecutive *Fox Swift* book. As always, she turned a potentially prickly process into a thoroughly enjoyable and collaborative one. 'BeeDub' (as she's known in DJ circles) not only has a keen eye for detail, but is also extremely proactive, often coming up with comical suggestions and solutions. Kudos to the power of 12!

Thanks to the whole team at The Slattery Media Group, especially Courtney Nicholls, Sara Demas and Jeffrey Sickert. So much goes on behind the scenes to produce, market and distribute a book, and all your time and effort is greatly appreciated.

Again, the book was road-tested on a group of brutally honest young readers, so a huge thank you to (in no particular order) Sophie, Molly, Xander, Li, Ned, Eliza, Sammy, Louis, 'S-Dawg' (Sarah), Rosie (a.k.a Rosie McHusky), Jack, Sam, Harry, Angus, Louis, Sam, Charlie, Ella, Gus, Henry, 'Ly-Z' (Eliza), Nick, Evie and Toby.

To my older (though less mature) sister Liz: *muchus est in appeciadus*. (That's 'thank you' in fake Latin.) Thanks for your invaluable feedback on the first draft. Being the incredibly generous brother I am, I have decided to double your fee. To my younger sister Jacque, thanks for your IT and moral support. I don't know why my computer suddenly works whenever I call you for assistance. (#possiblyusererror)

ACKNOWLEDGEMENTS

Thanks very much to all the readers who sent in imaginative story ideas and such positive emails to Cyril, Jo and me—we really appreciate your support and look forward to hearing your thoughts on *Fox Swift and the Golden Boot*. And a big shout out to Hamish Peele for his joke about the atom. Thanks to Andrew 'Dangerman' Stephens for his junior coaching "intel", to Leah Christoforou for her physio advice, and to Jo's and my literary agent, Sheila Drummond. A very special thanks to all the incredibly talented Tiwi Island students who helped with the storyline for the chapters 3, 4 and 5. I can't name all of you—no, wait a minute, I can!

Pularumpi School: Michael, Damien, Bernard, Misman, Tina, Max, Peter, Kathleen, Sam, James, Darius, Darnelle, Jesse, Olivia, Joline, Kianna, Bruce, Chelsea, Jenny, Cedric, Caitlin, Jocky Boy, Isobella, Mickey, Robert Jnr, Transtian, Ashton, Marie, Sherry, Yvonne, Brayden, Clinton, Stanley, Demaga.

Tiwi College: Michael, Leroy, Brady, Maurice, Kingy, Pedro, John Michael, Warrick, Lachlan, Anthony, Kyle, Josh, William, Ethan, John, Mikey, Cedric, Paulinus, Patty, Peter, Ryan, Garfield, Dion, Robert, Mark and Brandan.

A massive thank you to the Indigenous Literacy Foundation (ILF) for flying me (and some other writers with real talent) up to meet these incredible kids. If you are looking for a worthwhile charity to support, I strongly recommend the ILF.

And finally, thanks to my mum and dad for ... pretty much everything.

DAVID LAWRENCE

David Lawrence is a comedy writer whose TV credits include *Talkin' 'Bout Your Generation*, *TV Burp* and *Hamish & Andy*. He runs the successful comedy business Laughing Matters with Jo Gill, is the author of *Fox Swift* and *Fox Swift takes on The Unbeatables*, and the co-author with Eloise Southby-Halbish of *Anna Flowers*. David's goal was to play 100 games with Essendon, but due to a general lack of ability, he currently remains stranded on 0.

JO GILL

Jo Gill is a comedy writer and performer whose credits include *Hey Hey It's Saturday*, *Talkin' 'Bout Your Generation*, *Comedy Inc.*, *Hamish & Andy*, *Comic Relief*, and three years as head writer for the Logies. Jo has never won a Brownlow Medal, but has drawn three of them.

ACKNOWLEDGEMENTS

CYRIL RIOLI

Cyril Rioli is one of the game's most exciting midfielders and small forwards. He made his debut with the Hawthorn Football Club in 2008, and was a member of the club's surprise premiership win in that first season, in which he played all 26 games. By the end of the 2014 season had played 133 games and kicked 179 goals for the Hawks. He is one of the game's finest tacklers, and is renowned for his goal assists. He is now a triple premiership player, having been part of Hawthorn's back-to-back triumphs in 2013 and 2014.

WHAT'S NEXT FOR FOX?

Send us your ideas on how Fox should spend his next adventure ...

askus@foxswift.com.au

If you like Fox Swift's adventures with the Golden Boot, see where the story began!

Order at
www.foxswift.com.au

Also available from
Slattery Media

Order at
www.slatterymedia.com/store

AUTOGRAPHS

AUTOGRAPHS

AUTOGRAPHS

AUTOGRAPHS

AUTOGRAPHS

AUTOGRAPHS

I love your book so much that I have read it
13 times! It is a mind-catching book. You were so
lucky to write a book WITH Cyril Rioli. My favourite
character is Fox. You make the story come alive.
I really wish I was Fox. I love football ... At school we
have a day where we each dress up as a character from
a movie or a book—I dressed up as Fox Swift!

—Rosie

This is by far my favourite book ever. I came across
it last year and have read it several times since.
The first time I read it, I was so engaged by the story
that I couldn't put the book down.

—Mila (age 12)

I adore your funny and adventurous character,
Fox Swift ... I really hope that you write a whole series
about Fox Swift and his amazing friends.

—Thomas

I thought your book was fantastic! ... I read this
in the classroom every day and all of a sudden I just
started laughing and everyone stared at me.
That is how funny your book is.

—Alyssa

Read your book—amazing.

–Pranav

Your book is absolutely crazy ... I'm looking forward to reading book two 'cos I loved book one so much. I've never read a book better apart from one.

–Joey

Fox Swift was a great book, I loved it. It was so funny at times, like LOL funny! At the end it was very exciting and I learnt new things like how to kick grubber goals.

–Aki

I really like your book ... magnificent writing.

–Lachie

Your book is really good.

–Tom (age 9)

Fox Swift is awesome. Everyone I know loves it.

–Jacob

For my birthday I was given *Fox Swift* ... I enjoyed it very much, so much that I am currently re-reading it! I absolutely love books about footy and when I opened the package and read the blurb I was already engaged with Fox and the whole Swift crew. The thing I enjoyed the most was that Cyril Rioli helped give ideas and helped you write it. This for me was fantastic as it gave me some good training tips and he is one of my favourite players!

—Nick (age 13)

My brother lent me his *Fox Swift* book and I LOVED IT!!!

—Emma

We met you at the MCG signing a few weeks ago. My son Rex (then aged 6, now 7) had read your first book about 50 times. He read the second book in one day. He has now read it six times. He now sometimes sleeps with both books. Thought you would like to know. He has asked me to Google when the new book will be out. Now back to writing, please David!

—Lucy and Rex

I think you should make a movie out of the book so the world can know about AFL.

—Dom

Fox swift is a book that never tires me out.

—Hamish

Hi Fox and all his mates, Before the *Fox Swift* books were released I didn't really like reading, but you have changed my mind! I am sure you have heaps of fans, but personally I think I am one of your biggest! I hope there is heaps of twist turns and surprises in the third book and I CAN'T WAIT!
P.S. I LOVE THE *FOX SWIFT* BOOKS!!!
P.P.S. GO DIGGERS!!!
P.P.P.S. CAN YOU GET THE NEXT BOOK OUT SOON!!! P.P.P.P.S. HURRY UP PLEASE!!!

—Michael your biggest fan!

My son Dylan is loving the story and the tips he's getting along the way ... Thank you for such a brilliant book. It has certainly increased Dylan's interest in reading.

—Katrina

I have just read both of the books at school and I loved them.

—Max